Realization came to Deakin almost too late. He twisted his head around and peered forward into an opaque world filled with greyly driving snow.

Carlos, less than ten feet away, was crawling cautiously along the centre of the roof, knife in one hand and teeth gleaming in a smile in the dark face. With the same gleaming smile of wolfish satisfaction, he lifted his throwing hand over his shoulder. Deakin jerked his own right hand convulsively forward and the handful of frozen snow it held struck Carlos in the eyes. Blindly, instinctively, Carlos completed his knife throw, but Deakin had already flung himself forward in a headlong dive . . .

ALISTAIR MACLEAN

Breakheart
Pass

FONTANA/Collins

First published by Wm. Collins 1974
This Continental Edition first issued in Fontana Books 1975

© Alistair MacLean 1974

Made and printed in Great Britain by
William Collins Sons & Co Ltd, Glasgow

TO MARY MARCELLE

THE CHARACTERS

JOHN DEAKIN	A Gunman
COLONEL CLAREMONT	US Cavalry
COLONEL FAIRCHILD	Commandant of Fort Humboldt
GOVERNOR FAIRCHILD	The Governor of Nevada
MARICA FAIRCHILD	The Governor's niece and the daughter of Colonel Fairchild
MAJOR O'BRIEN	The Governor's Aide
NATHAN PEARCE	US Marshal
SEPP CALHOUN	A villain of some note
WHITE HAND	Chief of the Paiutes
GARRITTY	A gambler
REV. THEODORE PEABODY	Chaplain elect for Virginia City
DOCTOR MOLYNEUX	US Army Doctor
CHRIS BANLON	Engineer
CARLOS	Cook
HENRY	Steward
BELLEW	US Army Sergeant
DEVLIN	Brakeman on train
RAFFERTY	A trooper
FERGUSON	
CARTER	US Army Telegraphists
SIMPSON	
BENSON	
CARMODY	Three minor villains
HARRIS	
CAPTAIN OAKLAND	Passive but relevant
LIEUTENANT NEWELL	

The following bears very closely on the choice of 1873 as date for this story.

CALIFORNIAN GOLD RUSH	1855–75
COMSTOCK LODE DISCOVERED	1859
DISAFFECTED NEVADA INDIANS ACTIVE	1860–80
NEVADA BECAME STATE	1864
UNION PACIFIC RAILWAY BUILT	1869
BONANZA DISCOVERED	1873
CHOLERA IN ROCKIES	1873
DEVELOPMENT OF FIRST WINCHESTER REPEATERS	1873
UNIVERSITY OF NEVADA (ELKO) ESTABLISHED	1873
DISASTROUS FIRE IN LAKE'S CROSSING (WHICH BECAME RENO IN 1879)	1873

NB. It might appear odd that a US Army relief mission should be sent to attend a cholera outbreak, but this is not so: the State of Nevada Health Service was not established until 1893.

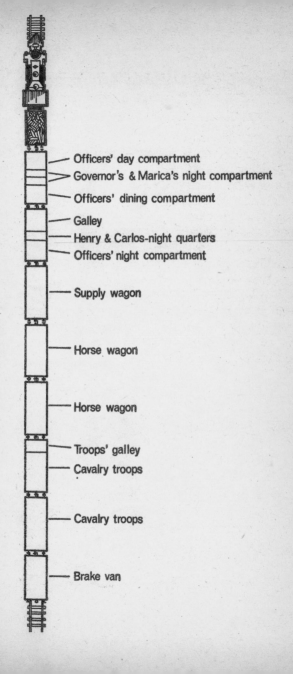

Officers' day compartment
Governor's & Marica's night compartment
Officers' dining compartment
Galley
Henry & Carlos-night quarters
Officers' night compartment

Supply wagon

Horse wagon

Horse wagon

Troops' galley
Cavalry troops

Cavalry troops

Brake van

ONE

The saloon bar of Reese City's grandiosely-named Imperial Hotel had about it an air of defeat, of uncaring dilapidation, of the hauntingly sad nostalgia for the half-forgotten glories of days long gone by, of days that would never come again. The occasionally plastered walls were cracked and dirty and liberally behung with faded pictures of what appeared to be an assortment of droop-moustached desperadoes: the lack of 'Wanted' notices below the pictures struck an almost jarring note. The splintered planks that passed for a floor were incredibly warped and of a hue that made the walls appear relatively freshly painted: much missed-at spittoons were much in evidence, while there were few square inches without their cigar butts: those lay about in their hundreds, the vast majority bearing beneath them charred evidence to the fact that their owners hadn't bothered to stub them out either before or after dropping them to the floor. The shades of the oil-lamps, like the murky roof above, were blackened by soot, the full-length mirror behind the bar was fly-blown and filthy. For the weary traveller seeking a haven of rest, the saloon bar offered nothing but a total lack of hygiene, an advanced degree of decadence and an almost stultifying sense of depression and despair.

Neither did the majority of the customers. They were remarkably in keeping with the general ambience of the saloon. Most of them were disproportionately elderly, markedly dispirited, unshaven and shabby, all but a lonely few contemplating the future, clearly a bleak and hopeless one, through the bottoms of their whisky glasses. The solitary barman, a myopic individual with a chest-high apron which, presumably to cope with laundry problems, he'd prudently had dyed black in the distant past, appeared to share in the general malaise: wielding a venerable hand-towel in which some faint traces of near-white could with difficulty be distinguished, he was gloomily attempting the impossible task of polishing a sadly cracked and chipped glass, his ultra-slow movements those of an arthritic zombie. Between the Imperial Hotel and, also of that precise day and age, the Dickensian concept of a roistering, hospitable and heart-warming coaching inn of Victorian England lay a gulf of unbridgeable immensity.

In all the saloon there was only one isolated oasis of conversational life. Six people were seated round a table close by the door, three of them in a high-backed bench against the wall: the central figure of those three was unquestionably the dominant one at the table. Tall and lean, deeply tanned and with the heavily crow-footed eyes of a man who has spent too long in the sun, he was dressed in the uniform of a colonel of the United States Cavalry, was aged about fifty, was – unusually for that time – clean-shaven and had an aquiline and intelligent face crowned by a mass of brushed-back silver hair. He wore, at that moment, an expression that could hardly be described as encouraging.

The expression was directed at a man standing opposite him on the other side of the table, a tall and powerfully built individual with a darkly saturnine expression and a black hairline moustache. He was dressed entirely in black. His badge of office, that of a US Marshal, glittered on his chest. He said: 'But surely, Colonel

Claremont, in circumstances such as those – '

'Regulations are regulations.' Claremont's voice, though civil enough, was sharp and incisive, an accurate reflection of the man's appearance. 'Army business is army business. Civilian business is civilian business. I'm sorry, Marshal – ah – '

'Pearce. Nathan Pearce.'

'Of course. Of course. My apologies. I should have known.' Claremont shook his head regretfully, but there was no trace of regret in his voice. 'Ours is an army troop train. No civilians aboard – except by special permission from Washington.'

Pearce said mildly : 'But couldn't we all be regarded as working for the Federal government?'

'By army definitions, no.'

'I see.' Pearce clearly didn't see at all. He looked slowly, thoughtfully, around the other five – one of them a young woman : none wore uniform. Pearce centred his gaze on a small, thin, frock-coated individual with a preacher's collar, a high domed forehead chasing a rapidly receding hairline and an expression of permanently apprehensive anxiety. He shifted uneasily under the Marshal's penetrating stare and his prominent Adam's apple bobbed up and down as if he were swallowing with considerable speed and frequency.

Claremont said drily : 'The Reverend Theodore Peabody has got both special permission and qualifications.' It was clear that Claremont's regard for the preacher was somewhat less than unlimited. 'His cousin is private secretary to the President. The Reverend Peabody is going to be a chaplain in Virginia City.'

'He's going to be what?' Pearce looked at a now positively cringing preacher, then unbelievingly at Claremont. 'He's mad! He'd last a damn sight longer among the Paiute Indians.'

Peabody's tongue licked his lips as he resumed his swallowing performance. 'But – but they say the Paiutes kill every white man on sight.'

'Not on sight. They tend to take their time about it.' Pearce moved his eyes again. Seated beyond the by now plainly scared pastor was a massively rotund figure in a loudly checked suit. He had the jowls to match his build, an expansive smile and a booming voice.

'Dr Edward Molyneux, at your service, Marshal.'

'I suppose you're going to Virginia City, too. Plenty work for you there, Doctor – filling out death certificates. Precious few from natural causes, I'm afraid.'

Molyneux said comfortably : 'Not for me, those dens of iniquity. You see before you the newly appointed resident surgeon for Fort Humboldt. They haven't been able to find a uniform to fit me yet.'

Pearce nodded, passed up several obvious comments and shifted his eyes again. A degree of irritation creeping into his voice, Claremont said : 'I may as well save you the labour of individual interrogation. Not that you have the right to know. A matter of courtesy, only.' Whether rebuke was either intended or accepted was impossible to say. Claremont gestured to the man seated on his right, a splendidly patriarchal figure with flowing white hair, moustache and beard who could have moved in and taken his place in the US Senate without having an eyelid batted in his general direction. Beard apart, the overall resemblance to Mark Twain was quite startling. Claremont said : 'Governor Fairchild of Nevada you will know.' Pearce inclined his head, then looked with a slight trace of interest at the young woman seated to Claremont's left. Perhaps in her mid-twenties, she had a pale face, strangely dark smoky eyes and her tightly drawn hair – or what little could be seen of it under a grey and wide-brimmed felt hat – was as dark as night. She sat huddled under a matching grey coat: the proprietor of the Imperial Hotel did not regard his profit margin as being of such an order as to justify any extravagant drain on the fuel supply for his corded wood stove. Claremont said: 'Miss Marica Fairchild, the Governor's niece.'

'Ah!' Pearce looked from her to the Colonel. 'The new quarter-master sergeant?'

Claremont said shortly: 'She's joining her father, the Commanding Officer at Fort Humboldt. Senior officers do have that privilege.' He gestured to his left. 'The Governor's aide and liaison officer to the Army, Major Bernard O'Brien. Major O'Brien – '

He broke off and looked curiously at Pearce. Pearce, in turn, was staring at O'Brien, a burly, sun-tanned, cheerfully plump-faced man. O'Brien returned the look with growing interest, then, with the almost immediate coming of recognition, jumped to his feet. Suddenly, both men, smiling widely, moved quickly towards each other and shook hands – four-handed – like long-lost brothers, before pounding each other on the back. The ancient regulars of the Imperial Hotel gazed upon the scene with wonderment: none of those present could ever recall Marshal Nathan Pearce displaying even a slight degree of emotion before.

Delight was in O'Brien's face. 'Sergeant Pearce! Why did it never ring a bell? *The* Nathan Pearce! I'd never have recognized you. Why, man, at Chattanooga your beard was – '

'Was nearly as long as your own, Lieutenant.'

'Major.' O'Brien spoke in mock severity, then added sadly: 'Promotion comes slowly, but it comes. Nathan Pearce, eh? The greatest army scout, the finest Indian fighter, the best gun – '

Pearce's voice was dry. 'Except for yourself, Major, except for yourself. Remember that day . . .' Arms around each other's shoulders and apparently quite oblivious of the rest of the company, the two men moved purposefully towards the bar, so profoundly an architectural monstrosity in design as to be deserving of a certain grudging admiration for its shoddy magnificence. It consisted of three enormous, and presumably enormously heavy, railway sleepers resting unsecured on a pair of trestles that seemed incapable of bearing a fraction of the weight they were being called upon to do. Originally, the classic simplicity of this design had been obscured by green linoleum on top and a floor-length drapery of velvet that had surrounded three sides. But time had had its inevitable way with both linoleum and velvet and the secrets of the designer were there for all to see. But despite the fragility of its construction, Pearce did not hesitate to lean his elbows on the bar and make appropriate signals to the glass-polisher. The two men fell into a low-voiced conversation.

The five who still remained at the table by the door remained silent for some time, then Marica Fairchild said in some puzzlement: 'What did the Marshal mean by "except for yourself"? I mean, they were talking about scouting and fighting Indians and shooting and, well, all the Major can do is fill in forms, sing Irish songs, tell those awful stories of his and – and – '

'And kill people more efficiently than any man I ever knew. Agreed, Governor?'

'Agreed.' The Governor laid his hand on his niece's forearm. 'O'Brien, my dear, was one of the most highly decorated Union Army officers in the War between the States. His – ah – expertise with either a rifle or hand

14

gun has to be seen to be believed. Major O'Brien is my aide, agreed, but an aide of a very special kind. Up in those mountain states politics – and, after all, I *am* a politician – tend to assume a rather – what shall we say? – physical aspect. But as long as Major O'Brien is around the prospects of violence leave me unconcerned.'

'People would harm you? You mean that you have enemies?'

'Enemies!' The Governor didn't exactly snort but he came pretty close to it. 'Show me a Governor west of the Mississippi who says he hasn't and I'll show you an out-and-out liar.'

Marica looked at him uncertainly, then at the broad back of O'Brien at the bar, the disbelief in her face deepening. She made to speak, then changed her mind as O'Brien and Pearce, glasses in their hands, turned away from the bar and made their way back to their table. They were talking earnestly now, Pearce obviously in some exasperation: O'Brien was trying to be conciliatory.

Pearce said: 'But damn it, O'Brien, you know what this man Sepp Calhoun is like. He's killed, robbed both stage companies and the railroad, fomented range wars, sold guns and whisky to the Indians – '

'We all know what he's like.' O'Brien was being very pacific. 'If ever a man deserved to hang, it's Calhoun. And hang he will.'

'Not until a lawman gets his hands on him. And *I'm* the lawman, not you and your lot. And he's up there now! In custody. In Fort Humboldt. All I want to do is to fetch him back. Up with your train, back with the next.'

'You heard what the Colonel said, Nathan.' Awkward and ill at ease, O'Brien turned to Claremont. 'Do you

15

think we could have this criminal sent back to Reese City under armed escort, sir?'

Claremont didn't hesitate. 'That can be arranged.'

Pearce looked at him and said coldly: 'I thought you said this wasn't army business.'

'It isn't. I'm doing you a favour. That way or no way, Marshal.' He pulled out his pocket watch and glanced irritably at it. 'Haven't those damned horses been watered and provisioned yet? God, if you want anything done in today's army you've got to see to it yourself.' He pushed back his chair and rose. 'Excuse me, Governor, but we're due to leave in half an hour. Back in a moment.'

Colonel Claremont left. Pearce said: 'Well, he doesn't pay the piper, the US tax-payer does that, but I suppose he calls the tune all the same. And half an hour?' He took O'Brien's arm and began to lead him towards the bar. 'Little enough time to make up for ten years.'

Governor Fairchild said: 'One moment, please, gentlemen.' He delved into a briefcase and held up a sealed package. 'Forgotten something, haven't we, Major?'

'Those old comrades' reunions.' He took the package and handed it across to Pearce. 'The Marshal at Ogden asked us to pass this on to you.'

Pearce nodded his thanks and the two men headed towards the bar. As they went, O'Brien looked casually around him: the smiling Irish eyes missed nothing. Nothing had changed in the past five minutes, no movement appeared to have been made: the ancients at the bar and tables might have been figures frozen for eternity into a waxen tableau. It was just at that moment that the outer door opened and five men entered and made for a distant table. They sat down and one of them produced a pack of cards. None of them spoke.

O'Brien said : 'A lively bunch of citizens you have in Reese City.'

'All the lively citizens – and by "lively" I include quite a few who had to be helped on to the saddles of their horses – left some months ago when they made the big Bonanza strike in the Comstock Lode. All that's left now are the old men – and God knows there are few enough of those around, growing old is not much of a habit in these parts – the drifters and the drunks, the shiftless and the ne'er-do-wells. Not that I'm complaining. Reese City needs a peace-keeping Marshal as much as the local cemetery does.' He sighed, held up two fingers to the barman, produced a knife, sliced open the package that O'Brien had given him, extracted a bunch of very badly illustrated 'Wanted' notices and smoothed them out on the cracked linoleum of the bar-top.

O'Brien said : 'You don't seem very enthusiastic.'

'I'm not. Most of them arrive in Mexico six months before their pictures are circulated. Usually the wrong pictures of the wrong men, anyway.'

The Reese City railroad station building was in approximately the same state of decrepitude as the saloon bar of the Imperial Hotel. The scorching summers and sub-zero winters of the mountains had had their way with the untreated clapboard walls and, although not yet four years old, the building looked to be in imminent danger of falling to pieces. The gilt-painted sign REESE CITY was so blistered and weather-beaten as to be practically indecipherable.

Colonel Claremont pushed aside a sheet of canvas that had taken the place of a door long parted with its rusted-through hinges and called out for attention. There was no reply. Had the Colonel been better acquainted with the ways of life in Reese City he would have found little occasion for surprise in this, for apart from the time devoted to sleeping and eating and supervising the arrival and departure of trains – rare occasions, those, of which he was amply forewarned by friendly telegraph operators up and down the line – the station-master, the Union Pacific Railway's sole employee in Reese City, was invariably to be found in the back room of the Imperial Hotel steadily consuming whisky as if it cost him nothing, which in fact it didn't. There was an amicable but unspoken agreement between hotel proprietor and station-master: although all the hotel's liquor supplies came by rail from Ogden, the hotel hadn't received a freight bill for almost three years.

Claremont, anger in his face now, pushed aside the curtain and went out, his eyes running over the length of his troop train. Behind the high-stacked locomotive and tender loaded with cordwood, were what appeared to be seven passenger coaches with a brake van at the end. That the fourth and fifth coaches were not, in fact, passenger coaches was obvious from the fact that two heavily sparred gangways reached up from the track-side to the centre of both. Standing at the foot of the first of the gangways was a burly, dark and splendidly moustached individual in shirt-sleeves, busy ticking items off a check-list he held in his hand. Claremont walked briskly towards him. He regarded Bellew as the best sergeant in the United States Cavalry while Bellew, in his turn, regarded Claremont as the finest CO he'd served under. Both men went to considerable lengths to conceal the opinions they held of each other.

Claremont nodded to Bellew, climbed up the first ramp and peered inside the coach. About four-fifths of its length had been fitted out with horse-stalls, the remaining space being given over to food and water. All the stalls were empty. Claremont descended the gangway.

'Well, Bellew, where are the horses? Not to mention your troops. All to hell and gone, I suppose?'

Bellew, buttoning up his uniform jacket, was unruffled. 'Fed and watered, Colonel. The men are taking them for a bit of a canter. After two days in the wagons they need the exercise, sir.'

'So do I, but I haven't the time for it. All right, all right, our four-legged friends are your responsibility, but get them aboard. We're leaving in half an hour. Food and water enough for the horses till we reach the fort?'

'Yes, sir.'

'And for your men?'

'Yes, sir.'

'Fuel for all the stoves, including the horse-trucks? It's going to be most damnably cold up in those mountains.'

'Plenty, sir.'

'For your sake, for all our sakes, there had better be. Where's Captain Oakland? And Lieutenant Newell?'

'They were here just before I took the men and the horses down to the livery stables. I saw them walking up to the front of the train as if they were heading for town. Aren't they in town, sir?'

'How the devil should I know? Would I be asking you if I did?' Claremont's irritation threshold was rapidly sinking towards a new low. 'Have a detail find them. Tell them to report to me at the Imperial. My God! The Imperial!'

Bellew heaved a very perceptible but discreetly inaudible long-suffering sigh of relief as Claremont turned away and strode forward towards the locomotive. He swung himself up the iron steps into the driving cab. Chris Banlon, the engineer, was short and lean almost to the point of scrawniness; he had an almost incredibly wrinkled, nut-brown face which made a highly incongruous setting for a pair of periwinkle blue eyes. He was making some adjustments with the aid of a heavy monkey wrench. Becoming aware of Claremont's presence, he made a last fractional adjustment to the bolt he was working on, returned the wrench to the tool-box and smiled at Claremont.

'Afternoon, Colonel. This is a privilege.'

'Trouble?'

'Just making sure there is none, sir.'

'Steam up?'

Banlon swung open the door of the fire-box. The blast of heat from the glowingly red-hot bed of cordwood made Claremont take a couple of involuntary steps backward. Banlon closed the door. 'Ready to roll, Colonel.'

Claremont glanced to the rear where the tender was piled high with neatly stacked cordwood. 'Fuel?'

'Enough to last to the first depot. More than enough.' Banlon glanced at the tender with pride. 'Henry and I filled every last corner. A grand worker is Henry.'

'Henry? The steward?' The frown was in Claremont's voice, not on his face. 'And your mate – Jackson, isn't it? The stoker?'

'Me and my big mouth,' Banlon said sadly. 'I'll never learn. Henry asked to help. Jackson – ah – helped us after.'

'After what?'

'After he'd come back from town with the beer.' The extraordinarily bright blue eyes peered anxiously at Claremont. 'I hope the Colonel doesn't mind?'

Claremont was curt. 'You're railway employees, not

20

soldiers. No concern of mine what you do – just so long as you don't drink too much and drive us off one of the trestle bridges up in those damned mountains.' He turned to go down the steps, then swung around again. 'Seen Captain Oakland or Lieutenant Newell?'

'Both of them, as a matter of fact. Stopped by here to chat to Henry and me, then went into town.'

'Say where they were going?'

'Sorry, sir.'

'Thanks, anyway.' He descended, looked down the train to where Bellew was saddling up his horse and called : 'Tell the search detail that they are in town.'

Bellew gave a sketchy salute.

O'Brien and Pearce turned away from the bar in the hotel saloon, Pearce stuffing the 'Wanted' notices back into their envelope. Both men halted abruptly and turned as a shout of anger came from a distant corner of the room.

At the card table, a very large man, dressed in mole-skin trousers and jacket that looked as if they had been inherited from his grandfather, and sporting a magnificent dark red beard, had risen to his feet and was leaning across the table. His right hand held what appeared to be a small cannon, which is not an unfair description of a Peacemaker Colt, while his left pinioned to the surface of the table the left wrist of a man sitting across the table from him. The face of the seated man was shadowed and indistinct, being largely obscured by a high-turned sheepskin collar and a black stetson pulled low on his forehead.

The man with the red beard said : 'That was once too often, friend.'

Pearce brought up by the table and said mildly : 'What was once too often, Garritty?'

21

Garritty advanced the Peacemaker till the muzzle was less than six inches from the seated man's face. 'Slippery fingers here, Marshal. Cheating bastard's taken a hundred and twenty dollars from me in fifteen minutes.'

Pearce glanced briefly over his shoulder, more out of instinct than any curiosity, as the saloon bar door opened and Colonel Claremont entered. Claremont halted briefly, located the current centre of action within two seconds and made his unhesitating way towards it : to play the part of bit player or spectator was not in Claremont's nature. Pearce returned his attention to Garritty.

'Maybe he's just a good player.'

'Good?' Garritty appeared to smile but, behind all that russet foliage, his intended expression was almost wholly a matter for conjecture. 'He's brilliant – too brilliant by half. I can tell. You won't forget, Marshal, that I have been playing cards for fifty years now.'

Pearce nodded. 'You've left me the poorer for meeting you across the poker table.'

Garritty twisted the left wrist of the seated man, who struggled hopelessly to resist, but Garritty had more than all the leverage he required. With the back of the left wrist pressed to the table, the cards in the hand were exposed : face-cards all of them, the top being the ace of hearts.

Pearce said : 'Looks a pretty fair hand to me.'

'Fair is not the word I'd use.' Garritty nodded to the deck on the table. 'About the middle, Marshal . . .'

Pearce picked up what was left of the pack of cards and ruffled his way through them. Suddenly he stopped and turned up his right hand : another ace of hearts lay there. Pearce laid it face down on the table, took the ace of hearts from the stranger's hand and laid it, also face down, beside the other. Their backs were identical.

Pearce said: 'Two matching decks. Who provided those?'

'I'll give you one guess.' The overtones in Garritty's voice were, in all conscience, grim enough: the undertones were considerably worse.

'An old trick,' the seated man said. His voice was low but, considering the highly compromising situation in which he found himself, remarkably steady. 'Somebody put it there. Somebody who *knew* I had the ace.'

'What's your name?'

'Deakin. John Deakin.'

'Stand up, Deakin.' The man did so. Pearce moved leisurely round the table until he was face to face with Deakin. Their eyes were on a level. Pearce said: 'Gun?'

'No gun.'

'You surprise me. I should have thought a gun would have been essential for a man like you – for self-defence, if nothing else.'

'I'm not a man of violence.'

'I've got the feeling you're going to experience some whether you like it or not.' With his right hand Pearce lifted the left-hand side of Deakin's sheepskin coat while with his free hand he delved into the depth of Deakin's inside lining pocket. After a few seconds' preliminary exploration he withdrew his left hand and fanned out an interesting variety of aces and face-cards.

'My, my,' O'Brien murmured. 'What's known as playing it close to the chest.'

Pearce pushed the money lying in front of Deakin across to Garritty, who made no attempt to pick it up. Garritty said harshly: 'My money is not enough.'

'I know it isn't.' Pearce was being patient. 'You should have gathered as much from what I said. You know my position, Garritty. Cheating at cards is hardly a Federal

23

offence, so I can't interfere. But if I see violence taking place before my eyes – well, as the local peace-keeper, I'm bound to interfere. Give me your gun.'

'My pleasure.' The ring of ominous satisfaction in Garritty's voice was there for all to hear. He handed his mammoth pistol across to Pearce, glared at Deakin and jerked his thumb in the direction of the front door. Deakin remained motionless. Garritty rounded the table and repeated the gesture. Deakin made an almost imperceptible motion of the head, but one unmistakably negative. Garritty struck him, back-handed, across the face. There was no reaction. Garritty said: 'Outside!'

'I told you,' Deakin said. 'I'm not a man of violence.'

Garritty swung viciously and without warning at him. Deakin staggered backwards, caught a chair behind his knees and fell heavily to the floor. Hatless now, he remained as he had fallen, quite conscious and propped on one elbow, but making no attempt to move. Blood trickled from a corner of his mouth. In what must have been an unprecedented effort, every single member of the regular clientele had risen to his feet: together, they pressed forward to get a closer view of the proceedings. The expressions on their faces registered a slow disbelief ultimately giving way to something close to utter contempt. The bright red thread of violence was an integral and unquestionable element of the warp and woof of the frontier way of life: unrequited violence, the meek acceptance of insult or injury without any attempt at physical retaliation, was the ultimate degradation, that of manhood destroyed.

Garritty stared down at the unmoving Deakin in frustrated incredulity, in a steadily increasing anger which was rapidly stripping him of the last vestiges of self-control. Pearce, who had moved forward to forestall

Garritty's next expression of a clearly intended mayhem, was looking oddly puzzled : then the puzzlement was replaced by what seemed an instant realization. Mechanically, almost, as Garritty took a step forward and swung back his right foot with a clearly near-homicidal intent, Pearce also took a step forward and buried a none too gentle right elbow in Garritty's diaphragm. Garritty, almost retching, gasped in pain and doubled over, both hands clutching his midriff : he was having temporary difficulty in breathing.

Pearce said : 'I warned you, Garritty. No violence in front of a US Marshal. Any more of this and you'll be my guest for the night. Not that that's important now. I'm afraid the matter is out of your hands now.'

Garritty tried to straighten himself, an exercise that clearly provided him with no pleasure at all. His voice, when he finally spoke, was like that of a bull-frog with laryngitis.

'What the hell do you mean – it's out of my hands?'

'It's Federal business now.'

Pearce slipped the 'Wanted' notices from their envelope, leafed rapidly through them, selected a certain notice, returned the remainder to the envelope, glanced briefly at the notice in his hand, glanced just as briefly at Deakin, then turned and beckoned to Colonel Claremont who, without so much as a minuscule twitch of the eyebrows, walked forward to join Pearce and O'Brien. Wordlessly, Pearce showed Claremont the paper in his hand. The picture of the wanted man, little better than a daguerreotype print, was a greyish sepia in colour, blurred and cloudy and indistinct in outline : but it was unmistakably a true likeness of the man who called himself John Deakin.

Pearce said : 'Well, Colonel, I guess this buys me my

train ticket after all.'

Claremont looked at him and said nothing. His expression didn't say very much either, just that of a man politely waiting.

Pearce read from the notice: ' "Wanted: for gambling debts, theft, arson and murder." '

'A nice sense of priorities,' O'Brien murmured.

' "John Houston alias John Murray alias John Deakin alias" – well, never mind, alias a lot of things. "Formerly lecturer in medicine at the University of Nevada." '

'University?' Claremont's tone reflected the slight astonishment in his face. 'In those godforsaken mountains?'

'Can't stop progress, Colonel. Opened in Elko. This year.' He read on: ' "Dismissed for gambling debts and illegal gambling. Embezzlement of university funds subsequently discovered, attributed to wanted man. Traced to Lake's Crossing and trapped in hardware store. To cover escape, used kerosene to set fire to store. Ensuing blaze ran out of control and central part of Lake's Crossing destroyed with the loss of seven lives." '

Pearce's statement gave rise to a splendid series of expressions among onlookers and listeners, ranging from incredulity to horror, from anger to revulsion. Only Pearce and O'Brien and, curiously enough, Deakin himself, registered no emotion whatsoever.

Pearce continued: ' "Traced to railroad repair shops at Sharps. Blew up wagonload of explosives destroying three sheds and all rolling stock. Present whereabouts unknown." '

Garritty's voice was still a croak. 'He – *this* is the man who burnt down Lake's Crossing and blew up Sharps?'

'If we are to believe this notice, and I do believe it, this is indeed the man. We all know about the long arm of coincidence but this would be stretching things a bit too far. Kind of puts your paltry hundred and twenty dollars into its right perspective, doesn't it, Garritty? By the way, I'd pocket that money right now if I were you – nobody's going to be seeing Deakin for a long, long time to come.' He folded the notice and looked at Claremont. 'Well?'

'They won't need a jury. But it's still not Army business.'

Pearce unfolded the notice, handed it to Claremont. 'I didn't read it all out, the notice was too long.' He pointed to a paragraph. 'I missed this bit, for instance.'

Claremont read aloud : ' "The explosives wagon in the Sharps episode was en route to the United States Army Ordnance Depot at Sacramento, California." ' He folded the paper, handed it back and nodded. 'This makes it Army business.'

TWO

Colonel Claremont, whose explosive temper normally lay very close to the surface indeed, was clearly making a Herculean effort to keep it under control. It was just as clearly a losing battle. A meticulous and exceptionally thorough individual, one who cleaved to prescribed detail and routine, one who had a powerful aversion to the even tenor of his ways being interrupted, far less disrupted, and one who was totally incapable of suffering either fools or incompetence gladly, Claremont had not yet devised, and probably never would devise, a safety-valve for his only failing as an officer and a man. Not for him the gradual release of or sublimation for the rapid and rapidly increasing frustration-based anger that simmered just below boiling point and did all sorts of bad things to his blood pressure. In geological terms, he neither vented volcanic gases nor released surplus super-heated energy in the form of spouts and geysers: like Krakatoa, he just blew his top, and the results, at least for those in his immediate vicinity, were, more often than not, only a slight degree less devastating.

The Colonel had an audience of eight. A rather apprehensive Governor, Marica, chaplain and doctor stood just outside the main entrance to the Imperial: some little way along the boardwalk O'Brien, Pearce and Deakin were also watching the Colonel in full cry, although it was noticeable that Pearce had an even closer eye for Deakin than he did for the Colonel. The eighth member was the unfortunate Sergeant Bellew. He was rigidly at attention, or as rigid as one can be when seated on a highly restive horse, with his gaze studiously fixed on a point about a couple of light years beyond the Colonel's left shoulder. The afternoon had turned cold but Bellew was sweating profusely.

'Everywhere?' Claremont's disbelief was total and he made no attempt to hide it. 'You've searched *every-where*?'

'Yes, sir.'

'Officers of the United States Cavalry can hardly be a common sight hereabouts. Someone's bound to have seen them.'

'No one we talked to, sir. And we talked to everyone we saw.'

'Impossible, man, impossible!'

'Yes, sir. I mean, no, sir.' Bellew abandoned his rapt contemplation of infinity, focused his eyes on the Colonel's face and said, almost in quiet desperation: 'We can't find them, sir.'

The colour of the Colonel's complexion deepened to a dangerous hue. It required no great feat of the imagination to see that the lava of his fury was about to erupt. Pearce took a couple of hasty steps forward and said: 'Maybe I can, Colonel. I can pick twenty, thirty men who know every hole and corner in this town – and heaven knows there are not a great number of those. Twenty minutes and we'll find them. *If* they're here to be found.'

'What the devil do you mean – if?'

'What I say.' It was obvious that Pearce was in no placatory mood. 'I'm offering to be of assistance – and I don't have to offer. I don't expect a "thank you", I don't even expect an acceptance. A little courtesy would help, though. Yes or no.'

Claremont hesitated, his blood pressure fractionally easing. He'd been brought up short by Pearce's curt tone and had to remind himself, painfully and almost forcibly, that he was dealing with a civilian, one of that unfortunate majority over whom he had neither control nor authority. Claremont kept his contact with civilians to a basic minimum, with the result that he had almost forgotten how to talk to them. But the root cause of his temporary indecision was the galling and humiliating prospect that those unwashed and undisciplined derelicts of Reese City might succeed where his own beloved troops had failed. When he did reply it cost him a very considerable effort to speak as he did.

'Very well, Marshal. Please do that. And thank you. Departure time, then, twenty minutes. We'll wait down at the depot.'

'I'll be there. A favour in return, Colonel. Could you detail two or three of your men to escort the prisoner to the train?'

'An escort?' Claremont was openly contemptuous. 'Hardly, I would have thought, a man of violence, Marshal.'

Pearce said mildly: 'It depends upon what you mean by violence, Colonel. Where the violence involves himself – well, we've seen he's no lover of bar-room brawls. But on his past record he's quite capable of burning down the Imperial or blowing up your precious troop train the moment my back is turned.'

Leaving Claremont with this cheerful thought, Pearce hurried into the Imperial. Claremont said to Bellew: 'Call off your men. Take the prisoner down to the train. Have his hands tied behind his back and put him on an eighteen-inch hobble. Our friend here seems to have the habit of disappearing into thin air.'

'Who do you think you are? God almighty?' There was a trace, slight though the combination was, of self-righteous anger and quavering defiance in Deakin's voice. 'You can't do this to me. You're not a lawman. You're only a soldier.'

'Only a soldier. Why, you – ' Claremont held himself in check then said with some satisfaction : 'A twelve-inch hobble, Sergeant Bellew.'

'That will be a pleasure, sir.' It was obviously an even greater pleasure for Sergeant Bellew to have his and his Colonel's displeasure directed against a common antagonist, however innocuous that antagonist might seem, rather than have the Colonel's wrath directed against him personally. Bellew withdrew a whistle from his tunic, took a deep breath and blew three ear-piercing blasts in rapid succession. Claremont winced, made a gesture that the others should follow him and led the way down towards the depot. After about a hundred yards, Claremont, O'Brien by his side, stopped and looked back. There was issuing forth from the doors of the Imperial what must have been an unprecedented exodus in the annals of Reese City. The motley crew could hardly have been classified under the heading of the halt and the lame and the blind, but they came pretty close to qualifying for it.

Due to the fact that the dilution of their whisky with water would have brought immediate and permanent ostracism to any of the Imperial's devoted clientele, at least half of those who emerged had the rolling, weaving gait of a windjammer sailor who had spent too long at sea. Two of them limped badly and one, no soberer than the rest, was making remarkably good time on a pair of crutches; he at least had the support that the others lacked. Pearce joined them and issued what appeared to be a series of rapid instructions. O'Brien watched the grey-bearded band disperse in a variety of directions and slowly shook his head from side to side.

He said : 'If they were on a treasure hunt for a buried bottle of bourbon, I'd have my money on them any day. As it is –'

'I know, I know,' Claremont turned dispiritedly and resumed the trek to the depot. Smoke and steam were issuing profusely and Banlon, clearly, had a full head of steam up. The engineer looked out.

'Any signs, sir?'

'I'm afraid not, Banlon.'

Banlon hesitated. 'Still want me to keep a full head of steam up, Colonel?'

'And why not?'

'You mean – we're going to pull out with or without the Captain and the Lieutenant?'

'That's precisely what I mean. Fifteen minutes, Banlon. Just fifteen minutes.'

'But Captain Oakland and Lieutenant Newell –'

'They'll just have to catch the next train, won't they?'

'But, sir, that might be days –'

'At the moment, I'm hardly in the mood to worry over the welfare of the Captain and the Lieutenant.' He turned to the others and gestured towards the steps leading up to the front of the first coach. 'It's cold and it's going to be a damned sight colder. Governor, with your permission, I'd like Major O'Brien stay with me a little. Just until this fellow Deakin is brought along. Nothing against my own men, mind you, none better, but I don't trust them to cope with a slippery customer like Deakin. But I think the Major can cope admirably – and without exerting himself unduly. Just till Pearce gets back.'

O'Brien smiled and said nothing. Governor Fairchild

nodded his agreement, then hastily mounted the steps. Even in the past fifteen minutes the late afternoon had become noticeably colder.

Claremont nodded briefly to O'Brien, then slowly began to walk the length of the train, from time to time slapping his very English swagger-stick – his sole concession to individuality or eccentricity, it all depended upon how one viewed it – against his leather riding boots. Colonel Claremont knew next to nothing about trains but he had been born with an inspectorial eye and rarely passed up the opportunity of exercising it. Further, he was the commandant of the train and Claremont believed in keeping a close and jealous eye upon his own, however temporarily that property might remain in his keeping.

The first coach consisted of the officers' day compartment – that into which the Governor had so recently and thankfully disappeared – the night compartments for the Governor and his niece and, at the rear, the officers' dining saloon. The second coach consisted of the galley, sleeping quarters for Henry and Carlos who were steward and cook respectively, and the officers' night compartment. The third coach was the supply wagon, the fourth and fifth the horse wagons. The first quarter of the sixth wagon was given over to the troops' galley, while the remainder of it and all of the seventh coach was given over to the troops' accommodation. None the wiser for his tour of inspection, Claremont reached the brake van, then, hearing the sound of hooves, looked towards the front of the train. Bellew had rounded up his lost sheep : as far as Claremont could ascertain he had the entire cavalry detachment with him.

Sergeant Bellew himself was in the lead. He held loosely in his left hand a rope, the other end of which was looped round Deakin's neck. Deakin himself, because of the twelve-inch hobble, was forced to walk in a ludicrously fast, stiff-legged gait, more like a marionette than a human being. It was a shameful and humiliating position for any grown man to find himself in but it left Claremont totally unmoved. He paused just long enough to see O'Brien move out to intercept Bellew, then swung himself up the brake van's steps, pushed open the door and passed inside.

Compared to the chill outside, the atmosphere inside the brake van was close on stifling, almost oppressively hot. The reason for this was not far to seek : the cordwood-burning stove in one corner of the van had been stoked with such skill and devotion that its circular, removable cast-iron top glowed a far from dull red. To one side of the stove was a bin well stacked with cordwood : beyond that again was a food cupboard – if the cordwood bin was anything to go by, Claremont thought, the cupboard would be far from empty – and beyond that again was the massive brake wheel. To the other side of the stove was a massive and massively over-stuffed armchair then, finally, a mattress piled high with faded army issue blankets and what looked like a couple of bearskins.

Almost buried in the depths of the armchair and reading a book through a pair of steel-rimmed and steel-legged glasses was a man who could only, in all fairness to the ancient cliché, be described as a grizzled veteran. He had a four-day growth of white beard on his face; his hair, if hair he had, was invisible beneath what looked like a Dutch bargee's peaked hat, pulled low over the ears, no doubt to keep out the cold. He was cocooned in considerable but indeterminate layers of clothing, the whole topped off with an Eskimo-type anorak made from equally indeterminate furs. To defeat the ill intent of even the most cunning of draughts, a heavy Navajo blanket stretched from his waist to his ankles.

As Claremont entered, the brake-man stirred, courteously removed his glasses and peered at Claremont with pale blue watery eyes. He blinked in surprise, then said: 'This is indeed an honour, Colonel Claremont.' Although over sixty years had passed since the brake-man had made his one and only crossing of the Atlantic, his Irish brogue was still so pronounced that he could have left his native Connemara only the previous day. He struggled to rise – no easy task from the position into which he had wedged himself – but Claremont waved him to sit down. The brake-man complied willingly and cast a meaningful glance towards the opened door.

Claremont made haste to close it and said: 'Devlin, isn't it?'

'Seamus Devlin at your service, sir.'

'Bit of a lonely life you lead here, isn't it?'

'It all depends upon what you mean by lonely, sir. Sure, I'm alone but I'm never lonely.' He closed the book he had been reading and clasped it tight in both hands. 'If you want a lonely job, Colonel, it's up there in the driver's cab. Sure, you've got your fireman, but you can't talk to him, not with all that racket up front there. And when it's raining or snowing or sleeting you've got to keep looking out to see where you're going, so that you're either frying of freezing. I should know, I spent forty-five years on the footplate but I got a bit past it a few years ago.' He looked around him with some pride. 'Reckon I've got the best job in the Union Pacific here. My own stove, my own food, my own bed, my own armchair – '

'I was going to ask you about that,' Claremont said curiously. 'Hardly Union Pacific standard issue, I should have thought.'

'I must have picked it up somewhere,' Devlin said vaguely.

'Many more years to retirement?'

Devlin smiled, almost conspiratorially. 'The Colonel is very – what do you say? – diplomatic. Yes, that's right, diplomatic. Well, sir, you're right, I'm afraid I'm a mite old for the job but I kind of lost my birth certificate years ago and that made things a bit difficult for the Union Pacific. This is my last trip, Colonel. When I get back east, it's my grand-daughter's home and the old fireside for me.'

'May heaven rain cordwood upon you,' Claremont murmured.

'Eh? I mean, I beg the Colonel's pardon.'

'Nothing. Tell me, Devlin, how do you pass the time here?'

'Well, I cook and eat and sleep and –'

'Yes, now. How about sleep? If you're asleep and a bad corner or a steep descent comes up what –'

'No trouble, sir. Chris – that's Banlon the engineer – and I have what they call these days communication. Just a wire inside a tube, but it works. Chris gives half a dozen pulls, the bell rings in here and I give one pull back to show that I'm in the land of the living, like. Then he gives one, two, three or four pulls, all depends how much pressure he wants me to put on the wheel. Never failed yet, sir.'

'But you can't spend all your time just eating and sleeping?'

'I read, sir. I read a lot. Hours every day.'

Claremont looked around. 'You've got your library

pretty well hidden.'

'I haven't got a library, Colonel. Just this one book. It's all I ever read.' He turned the book he held in his hand and showed it to Claremont: it was an ancient and sadly battered family Bible.

'I see.' Colonel Claremont, a strictly non-churchgoer whose closest brushes with religion came in his not infrequent conducting of burial services, felt and looked slightly uncomfortable. 'Well, Devlin, let's hope for a safe trip to Fort Humboldt and a safe last passage back east for you.'

'Thank you, sir. Much obliged, I'm sure.' Devlin had resumed his steel spectacles and had the Bible opened even before the Colonel had the brake van door closed behind him.

Claremont walked briskly towards the front of the train. Bellew and half a dozen of his men were busy dismantling the horse wagon ramps. Claremont said: 'Livestock and men. All accounted for?'

'Indeed, sir.'

'Five minutes?'

'Easily, Colonel.'

Claremont nodded and continued on his way. Pearce appeared round the corner of the depot building and hurried towards him. Pearce said: 'I know you'll never do it, Colonel, but you really do owe Bellew and his men an apology.'

'No signs of them? None at all?'

'Wherever they are, they're not in Reese City. My life on it.'

Claremont's first reaction, oddly enough, had been one almost of relief – relief that Pearce and his derelict posse had not succeeded where his own men had failed. But now the full implication of their apparent desertion or unforgivably delayed absence returned with renewed force and he said without unclenching his teeth : 'I'll have them court-martialled and dismissed the service for this.'

Pearce looked at him speculatively and said : 'I never met them, of course. Like that, were they?'

'No, dammit, they weren't.' Claremont slashed viciously at the side of his riding boot and barely repressed his wince of pain. 'Oakland and Newell were two of the finest officers I've ever had serve under me. But no exceptions, no exceptions. Fine officers, all the same, fine officers – Come on, Marshal. Time we were gone.'

Pearce boarded the train. Claremont looked back to check that the horse wagon doors were closed, then turned and raised his hand. Banlon gave an acknowledging wave from his cab, moved inside and opened the steam regulator. The driving wheels slipped once, twice, three times; then they began to bite.

THREE

By dusk, the troop train had left Reese City and the level plateau on which it stood so far behind that both were completely lost to sight. The high plain had now given way to the foothills of the true mountain country and the train was climbing gently up a long, wide, pine-wooded valley, the undulations of the track following closely those of the rock-strewn river alongside which it ran. The heavens were dark, there was no trace of the after-glow of sunset that must have been hidden behind those lowering clouds; there would be no stars, that night, and no moon; the leaden sky promised only one thing – snow.

The occupants of the officers' day compartment, understandably enough, displayed a minimum of concern for the chill bleakness and plainly deteriorating weather in the world beyond their windows. Cocooned as they were in warmth and ease and comfort, it seemed not only pointless but downright wrong to dwell upon the rigours without. Luxury is a pervasive anodyne and, for what was supposed to be an army troop train, the officers' compartment was unquestionably very luxurious indeed. There were two deep couches with split arm-rests at the front and back, and several scattered armchairs, all splendidly upholstered in buttoned-down brushed green velvet. The embroidered looped-back window curtains, held in place by tasselled silken cords, were made of what appeared to be the same material. The carpet was rust-coloured and deep of pile. There were several highly polished mahogany tables in the vicinity of the couches and chairs. In the right-hand front corner was a liquor cabinet, which was clearly not there for the purposes of display. The entire compartment was bathed in a warm amber glow from the gimballed and gleaming copper oil-lamps.

There were eight occupants of the compartment, seven of them with glasses in their hands. Nathan Pearce, seated beside Marica on the rear couch, had a glass of whisky, while she held a glass of port wine. On the front couch, the Governor and Colonel Claremont, and in two of the three armchairs, Dr Molyneux and Major O'Brien all held whisky glasses. In the third armchair the Rev. Theodore Peabody had a glass of mineral water and an expression of righteous superiority. The only person without a refreshment of any kind was John Deakin. Apart from the fact that it would have been unthinkable to offer hospitality to a criminal of such note, he would in any case have found it physically impossible to raise a glass to his lips as both hands were bound behind his back. His ankles, too, were tied. He was sitting on the floor, most uncomfortably hunched, close by the passageway leading to the night compartments. Apart from Marica, who cast him an occasionally troubled glance, none of the others present appeared to feel that Deakin's presence there constituted a jarring note. On the frontier, life was cheap and suffering so commonplace as hardly to merit notice, far less sympathy.

Nathan Pearce lifted his glass. 'Your very good health, gentlemen. My word, Colonel, I never knew the army travelled in such style. No wonder our taxes—'

Claremont was curt. 'The army, Marshal, does not travel in such style. This is Governor Fairchild's private coach. Behind your back are the two sleeping compartments normally reserved for the Governor and his wife — in this case the Governor and his niece — and beyond that again their private dining compartment. The Governor has very kindly offered to let us travel and eat with him.'

Pearce raised his glass again. 'Well, bully for you, Governor.' He paused and looked quizzically at Fairchild. 'What's the matter, Governor? You look a mite worried to me.'

The Governor did, indeed, look a trifle worried. He seemed paler than usual, his face drawn, his lips compressed. He forced a smile, emptied and refilled his glass and attempted to speak lightly.

'Matters of state, my dear Marshal, matters of state. Life in the legislature is not all receptions and balls, you know.'

'I'm sure it's not, Governor.' Pearce's pacific tone turned to one of curiosity. 'Why are you along on this trip, sir? I mean, as a civilian –'

O'Brien interrupted. 'A governor has full military powers in his own state, Nathan. Surely you know that.'

Fairchild said pontifically: 'There are certain matters calling for my personal presence and attention in Fort Humboldt.' He glanced at Claremont, who gave a tiny shake of his head. 'More I can't say – not, that is, at the moment.'

Pearce nodded, as if satisfied, and did not pursue the topic. A silence, not wholly comfortable, fell over the compartment, and was interrupted only twice by the entrance of Henry, the tall, immensely thin and almost cadaverous steward, once to top up glasses, once to replenish the cordwood-burning stove. Deakin's head had fallen forward on to his chest and his eyes were closed: he was either shutting out the world around him or had genuinely fallen asleep, which would have been no mean feat for a man trussed as uncomfortably as he was and having to brace himself, however unconsciously, against the increasingly erratic movements of the coach. The train, having reached a comparatively level stretch, had picked up speed and was beginning to sway from side to side. Even in those plushly upholstered seats, the motion was becoming distinctly uncomfortable.

Marica said uneasily to the Governor: 'Must we go so fast, Uncle Charles? Why all the fearful hurry?'

Claremont answered for the Governor. 'Because the engineer, Miss Fairchild, is under orders to make the best speed possible. And because this is an army relief train, and we're late. The United States Cavalry does not like to be late – and we're already two days behind schedule.' He lifted his eyes as Henry entered a third time and loomed there, the very image of the melancholy dyspeptic to whom, apparently, life was an intolerable burden.

'Governor, Colonel. Dinner is served.'

The dining-room was small, holding only two four-seater tables, but was furnished to the same luxurious standards as the day saloon. The Governor, his niece, Claremont and O'Brien were seated at one table, Pearce, Dr Molyneux and the Rev. Peabody at the other. There were some bottles of both red and white wines on the table and, by some legerdemain known only to Henry, the white wine was actually chilled. Henry himself moved around with a quiet if lugubrious efficiency.

Peabody lifted an austere hand against Henry's offer of wine, turned his glass, in what was clearly intended to be a significant gesture, upside down on the tablecloth, then resumed gazing at Pearce with an expression of mingled awe and horrified fascination.

Peabody said: 'By coincidence, Marshal, both the doctor and I come from Ohio, but even in *those* distant parts everyone has heard of you. My word, it is an odd sensation. Peculiar, most peculiar. I mean, to be sitting here, in person, so to speak, with the most famous – ah – lawman in the West.'

Pearce smiled. 'Notorious, you mean, Reverend.'

'No, no, no! Famous, I assure you.' Peabody's assurances were made in a very hasty fashion. 'A man of peace, of God, if you want, but I do clearly appreciate that it was in the line of duty that you had to kill all those scores of Indians –'

Pearce said protestingly: 'Easy on, Reverend, easy on. Not scores, just a handful and even then only when I had to. And there was hardly an Indian among them, mostly white renegades and outlaws – *and* that was years ago. Today, I'm like you – I'm a man of peace. Ask the Governor – he'll bear me out.'

Peabody steeled himself. 'Then why do you carry two guns, Marshal?'

'Because if I don't, I'm dead. There are at least a dozen men, most of them recently released from the prisons to which I sent them, who would dearly love to have my head on a platter. None of them will pull a gun on me, because I have acquired a certain reputation in the use of a hand gun. But my reputation would offer me as much protection as a sheet of paper if any of them ever found me without a gun.' Pearce tapped his guns. 'Those aren't offensive weapons, Reverend. Those are my insurance policies.'

Peabody carefully hid his disbelief. 'A man of peace?'

'Now? Yes. I was an army scout once, an Indian fighter, if you like. There are still plenty around. But a man gets sick of killing.'

'A man?' Despite what he probably imagined as his poker face, the preacher was manifestly still unconvinced. 'You?'

'There are more ways of pacifying Indians than shooting holes in them. I asked the Governor here to appoint me Indian agent for the territory. I settle differences between Indians and whites, allocate reservations, try and stop the traffic in guns and whisky and see to it that the undesirable whites are removed from the territory.' He smiled. 'Which is part of my job as Marshal anyway. It's slow work, but I'm making a little progress. I think the Paiutes almost trust me now. Which reminds me.' He looked at the other table. 'Colonel.'

Claremont lifted an enquiring eyebrow.

'Might be a good idea to have the curtains pulled about now, sir. We're running into hostile territory, and there's no point in drawing unnecessary attention to ourselves.'

'So soon? Well, you should know. Henry! You heard? Then go tell Sergeant Bellew to do the same.'

Peabody tugged Pearce's sleeve. His face was a mask of apprehension. 'Hostile territory, did you say? Hostile Indians?'

'Mainly we just call them hostiles.'

Pearce's indifference served only to deepen Peabody's fears. 'But – but you said they trusted you!'

'That's right. They trust *me*.'

'Ah!' What this meant was not clear, nor did Peabody care to elaborate. He just swallowed several times in rapid succession and lapsed into silence.

Henry served them coffee in the day compartment while O'Brien displayed considerable efficiency in dispensing brandy and liqueurs from the liquor cabinet. With all windows tightly closed and the top of the stove beginning to glow a dull red, the temperature in the compartment had risen into the eighties, but no one seemed unduly perturbed about this. On the frontier, extremes of heat and cold were an inevitable part of the way of life and phlegmatically accepted as such. The green velvet curtains were closely drawn. Deakin had his eyes open and, propped on one elbow, seemed more uncomfortable than ever, but because discomfort, like heat and cold, was also an integral part of the frontier, he received, apart from the occasional vexed glance from Marica, scant attention and even less sympathy. After some desultory small-talk, Dr Molyneux put his glass on the table, rose, stretched his arms and patted a yawn to discreet extinction.

He said: 'If you will excuse me. I have a hard day ahead tomorrow and an oldster like me needs his sleep.'

Marica said politely: 'A hard day, Dr Molyneux?'

'I'm afraid so. Most of our medical stores in the supply wagon were loaded at Ogden only yesterday. Must have them all checked before we get to Fort Humboldt.'

Marica looked at him in amused curiosity. 'Why all the great hurry, Dr Molyneux? Couldn't it wait till you get there?' When he made no immediate answer she said smilingly: 'Or is this epidemic at Fort Humboldt, influenza or gastric influenza or whatever you said it was, already out of control?'

Molyneux did not return her smile. 'The epidemic at Fort Humboldt –' He broke off, eyed Marica speculatively, then swung round to look at Colonel Claremont. 'I suggest that any further concealment is not only pointless and childish but downright insulting to a group of supposedly intelligent adults. There was, I admit, a need for secrecy to allay unnecessary fear – well, if you like, understandable fear – but all those aboard the train are now cut off from the rest of the world, and will remain that way, until we arrive at the Fort where they're bound to find out –'

Claremont raised a weary hand to dam the flow of

45

words. 'I take your point, Doctor, I take your point. I suppose we may as well tell. Dr Molyneux here is *not* an Army doctor and never will be. And, by the same coin, he's not any ordinary run-of-the-mill general practitioner – he is a leading specialist in tropical diseases. The troops aboard this train are not relief troops – they are replacement troops for the many soldiers who have died in Fort Humboldt.'

The puzzlement on Marica's face shaded quickly into fear. Her voice, now, was little more than a whisper. 'The soldiers – the many soldiers who have died – '

'I wish to God, Miss Fairchild, that we didn't have to answer your questions as to why the train is in such a hurry or why Dr Molyneux is in such a hurry or the Marshal's question as to why the Governor is so anxious.' He squeezed his eyes with his hand, then shook his head. 'Fort Humboldt is in the grip of a deadly cholera epidemic.'

Of the Colonel's seven listeners, only two registered anything more than a minimal reaction. The Governor, Molyneux and O'Brien were already aware of the existence of the epidemic. Pearce lifted only one eyebrow, and fractionally at that; the semi-recumbent Deakin merely looked thoughtful; apparently he was even less given than Pearce to untoward displays of emotional reaction. To an outside observer the lack of response on the part of those five might have appeared disappointing: but this lack was over-compensated for by Marica and the Rev. Peabody: fear and horror showed in the former's face, a stunned and disbelieving shock in the latter's. Marica was the first to speak.

'Cholera! Cholera! My father – '

'I know, my child, I know.' The Governor rose, crossed to her seat and put his arm around her shoulders. 'I would have spared you this, Marica, but I thought that if – well, if your father were ill, you might like – '

The Rev. Peabody's recovery from his state of shock was spectacularly swift. From the depths of his armchair he propelled himself to his feet like a jack-in-the-box, his face a mask of incredulous outrage. His voice had moved into the falsetto register.

'How dare you! Governor Fairchild, how dare you! To expose this poor child to the risks, the awful risks, of this – this dreadful pestilence. Words fail me. I insist that we return immediately to Reese City and – and – '

'Return how?' O'Brien maintained a carefully neutral tone and expression. 'It's no easy feat, Reverend, to turn a train on a single track railway.'

'For heaven's sake, padre, what do you take us for?' Claremont's surging irritability couldn't have been more clearly demonstrated by the waving of a red flag. 'Assassins? Would-be suicides? Or just plain fools? We have provisions aboard this train to last a month. And aboard this train we will remain, all of us, until Dr Molyneux pronounces the camp free from the epidemic.'

'But you can't, you can't!' Marica rose, clutched Dr Molyneux by the arm and said almost desperately: 'I know you're a doctor, but doctors have as much chance – more chance – of catching cholera than anyone else.'

Molyneux gently patted the anxious hand. 'Not this doctor. I've had cholera – and survived. I'm immune. Good night.'

From his semi-recumbent position on the floor Deakin said: 'Where did you catch it, Doctor?'

Everyone stared at him in surprise. Felons, like little children, were supposed to be seen and not heard. Pearce pushed himself halfway to his feet, but Molyneux waved him down.

'In India,' Molyneux said. 'Where I studied the disease.' He smiled without much humour. 'At very, very close quarters. Why?'

'Curiosity. When?'

'Eight, ten years ago. Again why?'

'You heard the Marshal read out my wanted notice. I know a little about medicine. Just interested, that's all.'

For a few moments Molyneux, his face oddly intent, studied Deakin. Then he nodded briefly to the company and left.

'This,' Pearce said thoughtfully, 'isn't nice. The news, I mean. How many at the last count, Colonel? Of the garrison, I mean. The dead.'

Claremont glanced interrogatively at O'Brien, who was his usual prompt and authoritative self. 'At the last count – that was about six hours ago – there were fifteen. That is out of a garrison of seventy-six. We don't have figures as to the numbers stricken but still alive but Molyneux, who is very experienced in such matters, estimates, on the basis of the number of the dead, that anything between two-thirds and three-quarters of the remainder must be affected.'

Pearce said : 'So possibly there are no more than fifteen fit soldiers left to defend the fort?'

'Possibly.'

'What a chance for White Hand. If he knew about this.'

'White Hand? Your bloodthirsty chief of the Paiutes?' Pearce nodded his head and O'Brien shook his. 'We've thought of this possibility and discounted it. We all know about White Hand's obsessive hatred of the white man in general and the United States Cavalry in particular, but we also know that he's very, very far from being a fool. If he weren't, the Army or – ' O'Brien permitted himself a slight smile – 'our intrepid lawmen of the West would have nabbed him quite some time ago. If White Hand knows that Fort Humboldt is so desperately under-manned, then he'll know why and will avoid the Fort like the plague.' Another smile, but wintry this time. 'Sorry, that wasn't meant to be clever.'

Marica said shakily : 'My father?'

'No. Clear so far.'

'You mean – '

'I'm sorry.' O'Brien touched her arm lightly. 'All I mean is that I know no more about it than you do.'

'Fifteen of God's children taken to their rest.' Peabody's voice emerged from the depths of the sepulchre. 'I wonder how many more of those poor souls will have been taken from us come the dawn.'

'Come the dawn,' Claremont said shortly, 'we'll find out.' Claremont, clearly, was increasingly of the opinion that the padre was a less than desirable person to have around in circumstances such as these.

'You'll find out?' Again the millimetric raising of Pearce's right eyebrow. 'How?'

'There's no magic. We have a portable telegraph transmitter aboard. We clamp a long lead on to the railroad telegraph wires : that way we contact the fort to the west of Reese City – even Ogden – to the east.' He looked at Marica, who had turned away. 'You are leaving us, Miss Fairchild.'

'I'm – I'm just tired.' She smiled wanly. 'Not your fault, Colonel, but you're not the bearer of very good news.' She walked away, stopped by the passageway entrance and looked for a long, considering moment at Deakin, then swung round to face Pearce.

'Is this poor man to get nothing at all to eat or drink?'

'Poor man!' There was open contempt in Pearce's

voice but it was clearly directed at Deakin, not Marica. 'Would you like to repeat that, ma'am, to the relatives of the folks who died in the fire at Lake's Crossing? Plenty of meat on that ruffian's bones yet. He'll survive.'

'But surely you're not going to leave him tied up all night?'

'That's just what I intend to do.' Finality in the voice. 'I'll cut him free in the morning.'

'In the morning?'

'That's it. And not for any tender feelings I have for our friend here. By that time we'll be deep in hostile territory. He won't try to escape then. A white man, alone, unarmed and without a horse wouldn't last two hours among the Paiutes. A two-year-old could track him in the snow – and apart from anything else he'd just starve or freeze to death. And whatever else we don't know about Master John Deakin, we have learnt that he has a mighty high regard for his own skin.'

'So he lies there – and suffers – all night.'

Pearce said patiently : 'He's a murderer, arsonist, thief, cheat and coward. You make a mighty poor choice for your pity, ma'am.'

'And you make a mighty poor example of a lawman, Mr Pearce.' Judging by the rather more than mildly astonished looks on the faces of the listeners, her stormy outburst was clearly out of character. 'Or don't you know the law? No, Uncle, I will not "shush, my dear". The law of the United States is very explicit on this. A man is innocent until proved guilty, but Mr Pearce has already tried, convicted and condemned this man and will probably hang him from the first convenient tree. The law! Show me the law that says that you're entitled to treat a man like a wild dog!'

With a swirl of her long skirts Marica made an angry

departure. O'Brien said, poker-faced: 'I thought you knew about the law, Nathan?'

Pearce scowled at him, then grinned ruefully and reached for his glass.

On the western horizon the dark clouds had now turned to a threatening indigo-black. The dimly-seen and still distant peaks loomed palely white against the ominous backdrop: the upper pines in the valley, along the foot of which the railway track snaked in conformation with the winding and partially frozen river, were already covered with snow. The relief train, scarcely more than crawling up the steep gradient, was moving into the bitter cold, the icy darkness of the uplands.

The contrast aboard the train itself could hardly have been more marked, but Deakin, alone now in the officers' day compartment, was hardly in a mood to appreciate this. The warmth from the cordwood stove, the warm glow from the single gimballed oil-lamp were clearly not the matters uppermost in his mind. He was still in his recumbent position but had now fallen over completely on his side. He grimaced in pain as he made another wrenching but futile attempt to ease the ropes that bound his wrists together behind his back; the brief attempt ceased as abruptly as it had begun.

Deakin was not the only one in that coach who was not asleep. Marica sat upright on the narrow bunk which occupied more than half of her tiny cubicle, thoughtfully biting her lower lip and glancing occasionally and irresolutely at her door. Her thoughts were centred on precisely the same matter as was engaging the attention of Deakin himself – the uncomfortable predicament in which the latter found himself. Suddenly, decisively, she rose, pulled a wrap around her and moved silently out into the passageway, closing the door as silently behind her.

She put her ear against the door next her own. It was clear that, within, silence was not at a premium : judging from the stentorian snores, the Governor of the State of Nevada had decided to let tomorrow's troubles look after themselves. Satisfied, Marica moved on, opened the door to the day compartment, closed it behind her and looked down at Deakin. He returned her gaze, his face giving away nothing. Marica forced herself to speak in a calm and detached manner.

'Are you all right?'

'Well, well.' Deakin looked at her with an expression of faint interest in his face. 'Perhaps the Governor's niece isn't quite the cocooned little marshmallow she seems to be. You know what the Governor or the Colonel or, for that matter, Pearce would do to you if you were found here?'

'And what would they do to me?' A degree of acerbity was not lacking in her voice. 'I hardly think, Mr Deakin, that you are in a position to warn or lecture anybody. And I would remind you that today is today and not a hundred years ago and I can get by quite well, thank you, without any cotton-wool or rose-petals. I asked you if you were all right.'

Deakin sighed. 'That's it – kick a man when he's down. Sure I'm all right. Can't you see? I always sleep this way.'

'As a form of wit, sarcasm is wasted on me.' Her voice was cold. 'And it looks as if I'm wasting my time on you. I came to ask if I can get you something.'

'Sorry. No offence. John Deakin is not at his best. As regards your offer – well, you heard what the Marshal said. Don't waste your sympathy on me.'

'What the Marshal says goes in my left ear and out the

right.' She ignored the slight surprise, the increasing interest in his face. 'There's some food left in the galley.'

'I've lost my appetite. Thanks, all the same.'

'A drink?'

'Ah, now! Did I hear the sound of sweet music?' He straightened, with difficulty, until he had reached a vertical sitting position. 'I've been watching them drinking all evening and it hasn't been pleasant. I don't like being spoon-fed. Could you untie the ropes on my wrists?'

'Could I – do I *look* mad? If once you got your hands free, you – you – '

'Would wrap them round your lovely neck?' He peered more closely at her neck while she regarded him in stony silence. 'It *is* rather lovely. However, that's hardly the point. At this moment, I doubt whether I could wrap my two hands round a whisky glass. Have you seen my hands?'

He twisted round and let her see them. They were blue and almost grotesquely swollen, with the thongs cutting deeply into the badly puffed flesh of the wrists. Deakin said : 'Whatever else our Marshal lacks, you must admit he brings a certain enthusiasm to the task on hand.'

Marica's face was tight-lipped, both anger and compassion in her eyes. She said : 'Do you promise – '

'My turn now. Do *I* look mad. Escape? With all those nasty Paiutes out there. I'd rather take my chance on the Governor's rot-gut whisky.'

Five minutes elapsed before Deakin could take that chance. It took Marica only a minute to untie him, but it took Deakin another four, after hopping to the nearest armchair, to restore a measure of circulation to his numbed hands. The pain must have been excruciating but his face remained immobile. Marica, watching him intently, said: 'I think John Deakin is a great deal tougher than everybody seems to give him credit for.'

'It ill becomes a grown man to bellow in front of a woman.' He flexed his fingers. 'I think you mentioned something about a drink, Miss Fairchild.'

She brought him a glass of whisky. Deakin drained half of it in one gulp, sighed in satisfaction, replaced the glass on the table by his side, stooped and started to free the ropes binding his ankles. Marica jumped to her feet, her fists clenched, her eyes mad; she remained like that for the briefest of moments, then ran from the compartment. She was back in seconds while Deakin was still untying his ankles. He looked in disfavour at the small but purposeful-looking pearl-handled pistol in her hand. He said: 'What are you carrying that around for?'

'Uncle said that if the Indians ever got me –' She broke off, her face furious. 'Damn you! Damn you! You promised me –'

'When a person's a murderer, arsonist, thief, cheat and coward, you can hardly be surprised when he turns out to be a liar as well. In fact, you'd be a damned idiot to expect anything else.' He removed the thongs from his ankles, pushed himself rather shakily to his feet, advanced two steps and casually removed the gun from her hand as if she had no intention of firing it, which she clearly hadn't. He pushed her gently down into an armchair, placed the little pistol on her lap, hobbled back to his chair and sat down, wincing briefly. 'Rest easy, lady. As it so happens, I'm not going anywhere. A little circulation trouble, that's all. Would you like to see my ankles?'

'No!' She was obviously seething with anger at her own lack of resolution.

'To tell you the truth, neither would I. Is your mother still alive?'

'Is my –' The unexpected question had caught her completely off-balance. 'What on earth has that to do with you?'

'Making conversation. You know how difficult it is when two strangers meet for the first time.' He rose again and paced gingerly up and down, glass in hand. 'Well, is she?'

Marica was curt. 'Yes.'

'But not well?'

'How would you know that? Besides, what business is it of yours?'

'None. Just that I'm possessed of an incorrigible degree of curiosity.'

'Fancy words.' It was questionable whether Marica was capable of sneering but she came very close to it. 'Very fancy, Mr Deakin.'

'I used to be a university lecturer. Very important to impress upon your students that you're smarter than they are. I used big words. So. Your mother is not well. If she were it would be much more natural for a fort commandant to be joined by his wife rather than his daughter. *And* I would have thought that your place would have been by your sick mother. *And* it strikes me as very odd indeed that you should be permitted to come out here when there's cholera in the fort and the Indians are so restive. Don't those things strike *you* as odd, Miss Fairchild? Must have been a very pressing and urgent invitation from your father, though for God knows what reasons. The invitation came by letter?'

'I don't have to answer your questions.' But it was apparent that, nonetheless, the questions intrigued her.

'In addition to all my other faults the Marshal listed, I've more than my fair share of persistent impertinence. By letter? Of course it wasn't. It was by telegraph. All urgent messages are sent by telegraph.' Abruptly, he switched his questioning. 'Your uncle, Colonel Claremont, Major O'Brien – you know them all very well, don't you?'

'Well, really!' Marica had renewed her lip-compressing expression. 'I think it's quite intolerable –'

'Thank you, thank you.' Deakin drained his glass, sat and began to retie his ankles. 'That was all I wanted to know.' He stood up, handed her another piece of rope, then turned with his hands clasped behind his back. 'If you would be so kind – but not quite so tight this time.'

Marica said slowly : 'Why all this concern, this interest in me? I should have thought that you yourself had enough worries and troubles –'

'I have, my dear girl, I have. I'm just trying to take my mind off them.' He screwed his eyes as the rope tightened on his inflamed wrists. He said protestingly :
'Easy, now, easy.'

She made no reply, tightened the last knot, helped ease Deakin to first a sitting, then a lying position, then left, still without a word. Back in her own cubicle, she closed the door softly behind her, then sat on her bed for a long time indeed, her eyes unfocused but her face very thoughtful and still.

In the redly and brightly illuminated driving cab the face of Banlon, the engineer, was equally thoughtful as he divided his time and attention between the controls and peering out the side window to examine the track ahead and the skies above. The black mass of cloud, moving rapidly to the east, now obscured more than half the sky; in a very short time indeed the darkness would be as close to total as it could ever be in uplands where mountains and pines – and increasingly the ground itself – were overlaid with a blanket of white.

Jackson, the fireman, was as close a carbon copy to Banlon as it was possible to be – abnormally lean, dark-complexioned and with two enormous crows' feet that traversed his parchment face from the ears almost to the tip of his nose. Despite the cold, Jackson was sweating profusely : on steep gradients such as this, the continuous demand for a full head of steam gobbled up fuel almost as quickly as it could be fed into the cavernous maw of the fire-box, casting Jackson in the role of little less than a slave to a very demanding master. He heaved a last section of cordwood on to the glowing bed of coals, mopped his forehead with a filthy towel and swung the door of the fire-box shut. The immediate effect was to reduce the footplate to a state of semi-darkness.

Banlon abandoned the cab window and moved towards the controls. Suddenly there came a loud, metallic and very ominous rattle. Banlon addressed a series of unprintable epithets towards the source of the sound.

Jackson's voice was sharp. 'What's wrong?'

Banlon didn't answer at once. He reached swiftly towards the brake. There was a moment's silence, followed by a screeching, banging clamour as the train, with a concertina collisioning of bumpers, began to slow towards a stop. Throughout the train all the minority who were awake – with the exception of the bound Deakin – and most of the majority who had just been violently woken grabbed for the nearest support as the train ground to its jolting, shuddering, emergency stop. Not a few of the heavier sleepers were dumped unceremoniously on the floor.

'That damned steam regulator again!' Banlon said. 'I think the retaining nut has come off. Give Devlin the bell – brakes hard on.' He unhooked a feeble oil-lamp and peered at the offending regulator. 'And open the fire-box door – I've seen better glow-worms than this goddamned lamp.'

Jackson did what he was asked, then leaned out and peered back down the track. 'Quite a few folk coming this way,' he announced. 'They don't seem all that happy to me.'

'What do you expect?' Banlon said sourly. 'A deputation coming to thank us for saving their lives?' He peered out on his own side. 'There's another lot of satisfied customers coming up this way, too.'

But there was one traveller who was not running forward. A vague and palish blur in the darkness, he jumped down from the train, looked swiftly around him, stooped, scuttled swiftly to the track-side and dropped down the embankment to the riverside below. He pulled a peculiar peaked coonskin cap low over his forehead and started running towards the rear of the train.

Colonel Claremont, despite his pronounced and very recently acquired limp – he had been one of the heavier sleepers and the contact his right hip had made with the floor had been nothing if not violent – was the first to reach the driving cab. With some difficulty he pulled himself up to the footplate.

'What the devil do you mean, Banlon, by scaring us all out of our wits like that?'

'Sorry, sir.' Banlon was very stiff, very proper, very correct. 'Company's emergency regulations. Control failure. The retaining nut – '

'Never mind that.' Claremont tenderly rubbed his aching hip. 'How long will it take to fix? All damned night, I suppose.'

Banlon permitted himself the faint smile of the expert. 'Five minutes, no more.'

While Banlon was bringing his expertise to bear, the running figure with the coonskin cap stopped abruptly at the base of a telegraph pole. He looked back the way he had come: the rear of the train was at least sixty yards away. Apparently satisfied, the man produced a long belt, passed it around himself and the pole and swiftly began to climb. Arrived at the top, he produced from his pocket a pair of wire-cutters with which he rapidly nipped through the telegraph wires on the side of the insulators remote from the train. The wires dropped away into the gloom and, almost as quickly, the man slid down to the ground.

On the footplate Banlon straightened, spanner still in hand. Claremont said: 'Fixed?'

Banlon raised a grimy hand to cover a prodigious yawn. 'Fixed.'

Claremont spared some of the concern for his aching hip. He said: 'You sure you're fit to drive for the rest of the night?'

'Hot coffee. That's all we need – and we have all the means and the makings right here in the cab. But if you could have Jackson and me spelled tomorrow – '

'I'll see to that.' Claremont spoke curtly, not from any animosity he held towards Banlon, it was merely that the pain in his hip was clamouring for his attention again. He climbed stiffly down to the track-side, made his way down the left side of the train and climbed as stiffly up the iron steps towards the entrance to the leading coach. The train slowly got under way again. As it did so, the coonskin-hatted figure appeared over the embankment to the right of the now moving train, glanced fore and aft, moved quickly forward and swung aboard the rear end of the third coach.

FOUR

Dawn came and it came late, as dawn does in mountain valleys so late in the year and in those altitudes. The distant peaks of the previous evening were now invisible, even although measurably closer; the grey and total opacity of the sky ahead – to the west, that was – was indication enough that, not many miles away, snow was falling. And, as could be seen from the gentle swaying of the snow-clad pine-tops, the morning wind was steadily freshening. Some of the pools in the river, where the water was almost still, had ice reaching out from both banks to meet almost in the middle. The mountain winter was at hand.

Henry, the steward, was stoking the already glowing stove in the officers' day coach when Colonel Claremont entered from the passageway, passing the recumbent and apparently sleeping form of Deakin without so much as a glance. Claremont, his limp of the previous night apparently now no more than a memory, rubbed his hands briskly together.

'A bitter morning, Henry.'

'It's all that, sir. Breakfast? Carlos has it all ready.'

Claremont crossed to the window, drew the curtain, rubbed the misted glass and peered out unenthusiastically. He shook his head.

'Later. Looks as if the weather is breaking up. Before it does, I'd like to speak to Reese City and Fort Humboldt first. Go fetch Telegraphist Ferguson, will you? Tell him to bring his equipment here.'

Henry made to leave, then stood to one side as the Governor, O'Brien and Pearce entered. Pearce moved towards Deakin, shook him roughly and began to untie his knots.

'Good morning, good morning.' Claremont was radiating his customary efficiency. 'Just about to raise Fort Humboldt and Reese City. The telegraphist will be here shortly.'

O'Brien said : 'Stop the train, sir?'

'If you please.'

O'Brien opened the door, moved out on to the front platform, closed the door behind him and pulled an overhead cord. A second or two later Banlon looked out from his cab and peered backwards to see O'Brien moving his right arm up and down. Banlon gestured in return and disappeared. The train began to slow. O'Brien re-entered and clapped his hands against his shoulders.

'Jesus! It's cold outside.'

'Merely an invigorating nip, my dear O'Brien,' Claremont said with the hearty disapproval of one who has yet to poke his nose outside. He looked at Deakin, now engaged in massaging his freed hands, then at Pearce. 'Where do you want to keep this fellow, Marshal? I can have Sergeant Bellew mount an armed guard on him.'

'No disrespect to Bellew, sir. But with a man so handy with matches and kerosene and explosives – and I should imagine that it would be an odd troop train that didn't carry a goodish supply of all three of those – well, I'd rather keep a personal eye on him.'

Claremont nodded briefly, then turned his attention towards two soldiers who had just knocked and entered. Telegraphist Ferguson was carrying a collapsible table, a coil of cable, and a small case containing his writing material. Behind him his assistant, a young trooper called

Brown, was lugging the bulky transmitter. Claremont said: 'As soon as you're ready.'

Two minutes later Telegraphist Ferguson was ready. He was perched on the arm of a sofa, and from the telegraph set before him a lead passed through a minimally opened crack in the window. With his handkerchief, Claremont rubbed the misted window and peered out. The lead looped up to the top of a telegraph pole from which Brown was supported by a belt. Brown finished whatever adjustment he was making, then turned and waved a hand. Claremont turned to Ferguson. 'Right. The Fort first.'

Ferguson tapped out a call-up signal three times in succession. Almost at once, through his earphones, could be heard the faint chatter of Morse. Ferguson eased back his earphones and said: 'A minute, sir. They're fetching Colonel Fairchild.'

While they were waiting Marica entered, closely followed by the Rev. Peabody. Peabody was wearing his graveside expression and looked as if he had passed a very bad night. Marica glanced first, without expression, at Deakin, then, interrogatively, at her uncle.

'We're in touch with Fort Humboldt, my dear,' the Governor said. 'We should have the latest report in a minute.'

Faintly, the renewed sound of Morse could be heard from the earphones. Ferguson wrote, rapidly but neatly, tore a sheet from his pad and handed it to Claremont.

More than a day's journey away over the mountains, eight men sat or stood in the telegraphy room in Fort Humboldt. The central and unquestionably the dominating figure in the room lounged in a swivel chair behind a rather splendid leather-topped mahogany table, with both his filthy riding boots resting squarely on top of the desk. The spurs which he needlessly affected had left the leather top in several degrees less than mint condition, a consideration that apparently left the wearer unmoved. His general appearance attested to the first impression that there was little of the aesthetic about him. Even seated, it could be seen that he was a tall figure, bulky and broad-shouldered, with a ragged deerskin jacket pulled back to reveal a sagging belt weighted down by a pair of Peacemaker Colts. Above the jacket and below a stetson that had been old while the jacket was still in its first youth, a high-boned face, hooked nose, cold eyes of a washed-out grey and a week's growth of beard over-laying a naturally swarthy complexion gave one the impression of being in the presence of a ruthless desper-ado, which was, in fact, a pretty apt description for Sepp Calhoun.

A man dressed in United States Cavalry uniform was seated by the side of Calhoun's table, while several feet away another soldier sat by the telegraph. Calhoun looked at the man by his side.

'Well, Carter, let's see if Simpson really transmitted the message I gave him to translate.' Scowling, Carter passed the message across. Calhoun took it and read aloud: ' "Three more cases. No more deaths. Hope epidemic has passed peak. Expected time of arrival, please." ' He looked towards the operator. 'Takes a clever man not to be *too* clever, eh, Simpson? Ain't either of us can afford to make a mistake, is there?'

In the day coach Colonel Claremont had just read out the same message. He laid the note down and said: 'Well, that *does* make good news. Our time of arrival?' He glanced at O'Brien. 'Approximately.'

'To haul this heavy load with a single loco?' O'Brien pondered briefly. 'Thirty hours, I'd say, sir. I can check with Banlon.'

'No need. Near enough.' He turned to Ferguson. 'You heard? Tell them –'

Marica said : 'My father –'

Ferguson nodded, transmitted. He listened to the reply, eased his headphones and looked up. He said : 'Expect you tomorrow afternoon. Colonel Fairchild well.'

While Marica smiled her relief, Pearce said : 'Could you tell the Colonel I'm aboard, coming to take Sepp Calhoun into custody?'

In the Fort Humboldt telegraph room, Sepp Calhoun was also smiling, but not with relief. He made no attempt to conceal the wicked amusement in his eyes as he handed a slip of telegraph paper to a tall, grey-haired, grey-moustached Colonel of the United States Cavalry. 'Honestly, now, Colonel Fairchild, doesn't that beat everything! They're going to come to take poor old Sepp Calhoun into custody. Whatever in the world shall I do?'

Colonel Fairchild read the message and said nothing. His face expressed nothing. Contemptuously, he opened his fingers and let the message drop to the floor. For a moment Calhoun's eyes became still, then he relaxed and smiled again. He could afford to smile. He looked at the four men close to the doorway, two raggedly dressed white men and two equally unprepossessing Indians, all four with rifles pointed variously at Fairchild and the two soldiers, and said : 'The Colonel must be feeling hungry. Let him get back to his breakfast.'

Claremont said : 'Now try for the telegraph operator at the Reese City depot. Find out if he has any information for us about Captain Oakland or Lieutenant Newell.'

Ferguson said : 'The depot, sir? That'll be the station-master. I mean, they don't have a telegraph office in Reese City any more. They tell me the telegraphist left for the Big Bonanza some time ago.'

'Well, the station-master.'

'Yes, sir.' Ferguson hesitated. 'The word is, sir, that he's not seen at the depot very often. He appears to spend most of his life in the back room of the Imperial Hotel.'

'Try, anyway.'

Ferguson tried. He transmitted the call-sign at least a dozen times, then looked up. 'I don't seem to be able to raise them, sir.'

O'Brien said, *sotto voce*, to Pearce : 'Maybe they should switch the telegraph to the Imperial.' The tightening of Claremont's lips showed that the remark hadn't been quite so *sotto voce* as intended, but he ignored it and said to Ferguson : 'Keep trying.'

Ferguson tried and kept on trying. His earphones remained obstinately silent. He shook his head and looked towards Claremont, who forestalled him. 'No one manning the other end, eh?'

'No, sir, nothing like that.' Ferguson was genuinely puzzled. 'The line's out of action. Dead. One of the relay repeaters gone, most like.'

'I don't see how it can have gone. No snow, no high winds – and nothing the matter with any of them when we called the Fort from Reese City yesterday. Keep trying while we have some breakfast.' He paused, looked first of all unenthusiastically at Deakin, then in grieved enquiry at Pearce. 'This criminal here, this Houston. Does he have to eat with us?'

'Deakin,' Deakin said. 'Not Houston.'

'Shut up,' Pearce said. To the Colonel: 'He could starve for all I care – but, well, he can sit at my table. If the Reverend and the Doctor don't mind, that is.' He glanced around. 'I see the good Doctor isn't up and about yet.' He took Deakin none too gently by the arm. 'Come on.'

The seven people taking breakfast were seated as they had been the previous evening, except that Deakin had taken the place of Dr Molyneux, who had yet to put in an appearance. Peabody, seated next to him, spent what was clearly a most uncomfortable meal: he kept glancing furtively at Deakin and had about him the look of a divine on the *qui vive* for the emergence of a pair of horns and forked tail. Deakin, for his part, paid no attention: as befitted a man who had just undergone an enforced absence from the pleasures of the table, his undivided attention was devoted to the contents of the plate before him.

Claremont finished his meal, sat back, nodded to Henry to pour him some more coffee, lit a cheroot and glanced across at Pearce's table. He permitted himself one of his rare and wintry smiles.

'I'm afraid Dr Molyneux is going to find some difficulty in adjusting to army breakfast times. Henry, go and waken him.' He twisted in his seat and called down the passageway. 'Ferguson?'

'No luck, sir. Nothing. Quite dead.'

For a moment, head still averted, Claremont tapped his fingers irresolutely on the table, then made up his mind. 'Dismantle your equipment,' he called, then turned to face the company again. 'We'll leave as soon as he's ready. Major O'Brien, if you would be so kind – ' He broke off in astonishment as Henry, his measured steward's gait in startling abeyance, almost rushed into the dining-room, wide eyes reflecting the shock mirrored in the long lugubrious face.

'What on earth's the matter, Henry?'

'He's dead, Colonel! He's lying there dead! Dr Molyneux.'

'Dead? Dead? The doctor? Are you – are you sure, Henry? Did you shake him?'

Henry nodded and shivered at the same moment, then gestured towards the window. 'He's like the ice in that river.' He moved to one side as O'Brien pushed by. 'Heart, I'd say, sir. Looked as if he slipped away peaceful, like.'

Claremont rose and paced up and down in the narrow confined space available to him. 'Good God! This is dreadful, dreadful.' It was clear that Claremont, apart from the natural shock at the news of Molyneux's death, was aghast at the implications it held: but it was left to the Reverend Peabody to put it into words.

'In the midst of life . . .' For a person built along the lines of an undernourished scarecrow Peabody was possessed of an enormously deep and sepulchral voice that seemed to resonate from the depths of the tomb. 'Dreadful for him, Colonel, dreadful to be struck down in his prime, dreadful for those sick and dying souls in the Fort who were depending upon him, and him alone, to come to their succour. Ah, the irony of it, the bitter irony of it all. Life is but a walking shadow.' What was meant by the last remark was not clear and Peabody, it was equally clear, was in no mind to elucidate: hands clasped and eyes screwed tightly shut, Peabody was deep in silent prayer.

O'Brien entered, his face grave and set. He nodded in reply to Claremont's interrogative glance.

'Died in his sleep, I'd say, sir. As Henry says, it looks

like a heart attack, and a sudden and massive one at that. From his face, it seems that he never knew anything about it.'

Deakin said : 'Could I have a look?'

Seven pairs of eyes, including those of the Reverend Peabody, who had momentarily interrupted his intercession with the hereafter, immediately turned on Deakin, but none with quite the cold hostility of Colonel Claremont's.

'You? What the devil for?'

'Establish the exact cause of death, maybe.' Deakin shrugged, relaxed to the point of indifference. 'You know that I trained to be a doctor.'

'Qualified?'

'And disbarred.'

'Inevitably.'

'Not for incompetence. Not for professional misconduct.' Deakin paused then went on delicately : 'For other things, shall we say? But once a doctor, always a doctor.'

'I suppose so.' Claremont was sufficiently a realist to allow his pragmatism to override his personal feelings. 'Well, why not? Show him, Henry.'

A profound silence enveloped the dining compartment after the departure of the two men. There were so many things to be said, but all those things were so obvious that it appeared pointless to say them : by common consent they avoided the gaze of each other and seemed to concentrate on objects in the middle distance. Even the advent of Henry with another pot of fresh coffee failed to dispel the funereal atmosphere, if for no reason other than the fact that Henry was a natural for the chief mourner at any wake. All seven pairs of eyes withdrew their gazes from the far distances as Deakin returned.

Claremont said : 'Heart attack?'

Deakin considered. 'I guess you could call it that. Kind of.' He glanced at Pearce. 'Lucky for us we have the law aboard.'

'What do you mean, sir?' Governor Fairchild looked even more distraught than he had the previous evening: with what was possibly very good reason, he now looked positively distressed.

'Somebody knocked Molyneux out, took a probe from his surgical case, inserted it under the rib cage and pushed up, piercing his heart. Death would have supervened pretty well immediately.' Deakin surveyed the company in an almost leisurely fashion. 'I would say that it was done by someone with some medical knowledge, at least of anatomy. Any of you lot know anything about anatomy?'

Claremont's voice was forgiveably harsh. 'What in God's name are you saying?'

'He was struck on the head by something heavy and solid – like a gun butt, say. The skin above the left ear is broken. But death occurred before there was time for a bruise to form. Just below the ribs is a tiny blue-red puncture. Go see for yourselves.'

'This is preposterous.' Claremont's expression didn't quite match the expressed conviction, there was a disturbing certainty about the way in which Deakin spoke. 'Preposterous!'

'Of course it is. What *really* happened is that he stabbed himself to death, *then* cleaned up the probe and returned it to his case. Tidy to the end.'

'This is hardly the time –'

'You've got a murderer aboard. Why don't you go and check?'

Claremont hesitated, then led an almost concerted movement back towards the second coach, even the

Reverend Peabody pressing along anxiously if apprehensively in the rear. Deakin was left alone with Marica, who sat tensely in her chair, hands clenched in her lap and looking at him with a most peculiar expression. When she spoke it was almost in a whisper.

'A murderer! *You're* a murderer. The Marshal says so. Your Wanted notice says so. *That's* why you had me untie and tie those ropes, so that later you could wriggle out – '

'Heaven send me help.' Wearily, Deakin poured himself some more coffee. 'Clear-cut motive, of course – I wanted his job so I upped and did him in in the middle of the night. I killed him, faking to make it look like a natural death, then proved to everyone it wasn't. Then of course, I re-tied my hands behind my back, using my toes to tie the knots.' He rose, moved past her, touched her lightly on the shoulder, then moved on to a steam-clouded window, which he began to clear. 'I'm tired too. It's snowing now. The sky's getting dark, the wind's getting up and there's a blizzard lurking behind those peaks. No day for a burial service.'

'There won't be any. They'll take him all the way back to Salt Lake.'

'They'll do what?'

'Doctor Molyneux. *And* all the men who have died in the epidemic at Fort Humboldt. It's normal peacetime practice. The relatives and friends – well, they like to be there.'

'But it – it'll take *days* to – '

Not looking at him, she said: 'There are about thirty empty coffins in the supply wagon.'

'There are? Well, I'll be damned. A railroad hearse!'

'More or less. We were told that those coffins were going to Elko. Now we know they're going no further

70

than Fort Humboldt.' She shivered despite the warmth of the compartment. 'I'm glad I'm not returning on this train . . . Tell me, who do you think did it?'

'Did what? Ah, the Doc. Set a murderer to catch a murderer, is that it?'

'No.' The dark eyes looked at him levelly. 'I didn't mean that.'

'Well, it wasn't me and it wasn't you. That only leaves the Marshal with about seventy other suspects – I don't know how many troops they have aboard. Ah! Here are some of them coming now.'

Claremont entered, followed by Pearce and O'Brien. Deakin caught his eye. Claremont nodded heavily and, just as heavily, sat down in silence and reached for the coffee-pot.

As the morning progressed, so did the snow steadily thicken, as Deakin had predicted. The increase of the wind had not kept pace with that of the snow so blizzard conditions were still some way off : but all the signs were there.

The train was now fairly into the spectacular mountain country. The track no longer ran along valleys with rivers meandering through them, but through steep, almost precipitously-sided gorges, through tunnels or along permanent ways that had been blasted out of the solid rock leaving a cliff-edge drop to the foot of the ravine below.

Marica peered through a lee-side window that was relatively free from snow and thought, not for the first time, that those mountains were no place for the faint-hearted and advanced sufferers from vertigo. At the moment, the train was rattling and swaying its way across a trellis bridge spanning an apparently bottomless gorge, the lowermost supports of the bridge being lost in the gloomy and snow-filled ravine below.

As the locomotive came off the bridge, it curved away to the right and began to climb up the left-hand side of a steep-sided valley, towering snow-clad pines to the left, the ravine to the right. The brake van had just cleared the bridge when Marica staggered and almost fell as the train brakes screeched and jolted the train to a violent halt. None of the men in the dining compartment was similarly affected for the sufficient reason that they were all sitting down: but the explosive language of Claremont could be taken as being fairly representative of their general feelings. Within seconds, Claremont, O'Brien, Pearce and, more leisurely, Deakin had risen, moved out on to the rear platform of the leading coach and swung down to the ankle-deep snow of the trackside.

Banlon, his wizened face twisted with anxiety, came running down the track. O'Brien caught and checked him, Banlon struggled to free himself. He shouted: 'God's sake, let go! He's fallen off.'

'Who has, man?'

'Jackson, my fireman!' Banlon broke free and ran on to the bridge, stopped and peered down into the murky depths. He hurried on another few paces and looked again. This time he remained where he was, first kneeling and then lowering himself until he was prone on the snow. He was joined almost immediately by the others, including by now Sergeant Bellew and some soldiers. All of them peered gingerly over the edge of the bridge.

Sixty, perhaps seventy feet below, a crumpled figure lay huddled on a spur of rock. Over a hundred feet below that again the foaming white waters of the river at the foot of the gorge could dimly be discerned.

Pearce said: 'Well, Doctor Deakin?' The emphasis on the 'doctor' was minimal: but it was there.

Deakin was curt. 'He's dead. Any fool can see that.'

'I don't regard myself as a fool and I can't see it,' Pearce said mildly. 'He might be in need of medical assistance. Agreed, Colonel Claremont?'

'I have no power to ask this man —'

Deakin said: 'And neither has Pearce. And if I go down, what guarantee have I that Pearce won't arrange for a life-line to slip? We all know the high opinion the Marshal has of me and we all know that after my trial I'm for the drop. It would save the Marshal an awful lot of time and trouble if he were kind of accidentally to arrange for me to have this drop now — right down to the bottom of the gorge.'

'There'll be six of my soldiers belaying that rope, Deakin.' Claremont's face was stony. 'You insult me, sir.'

'I do?' Deakin looked at him consideringly. 'Yes, I do believe I do. My apologies.' He took the end of the rope, made a double bowline, thrust his legs through the loops and took a bight around his waist. 'I'd like another rope, too.'

'Another rope?' Claremont frowned. 'That one would support a horse.'

'I wasn't thinking so much about horses. Would you think it fitting for an army colonel to lie down there until the vultures picked you clean to the bone? Or is it only cavalrymen who rate a decent burial?'

Claremont bestowed a momentary blue glare on Deakin, whirled and nodded to Bellew. Within a minute a soldier had returned with a rope and within two more, after a dizzying, swaying descent, Deakin had secured a foothold on the spur of rock which held the broken body of Jackson.

73

For almost a minute, buffeted by the gusting winds down the ravine, Deakin remained stooped over the prone figure, then secured the second rope round Jackson. He straightened, lifted a hand in signal and was hauled back up to the bridge again.

'Well?' Predictably, the impatient Claremont.

Deakin undid his rope and rubbed two painfully grazed knees. 'Fractured skull, nearly every major rib in his body broken.' He looked enquiringly at Banlon. 'He had a rag tied to his right wrist.'

'That's right.' Banlon appeared to have shrunk another impossible inch or two. 'He was outside, clearing the snow from my driving window, when he fell off. Tying the rag like that is an old fireman's trick. He can hang on with both hands.'

'Didn't hang on this time, did he? I think I know why. Marshal, you'd better come – as law officer you'll be asked to certify the death certificate. Disbarred doctors are denied that privilege.'

Pearce hesitated, nodded and moved off after Deakin, O'Brien following close behind. Deakin reached the locomotive, walked a couple of paces past the cab and looked up. The snow in the vicinity of the engineer's window and on the after part of the boiler casing had been rubbed off. Deakin swung up to the cab and, watched by Pearce, O'Brien and Banlon, who had now joined them, looked first around him and then behind him. The tender was now two-thirds empty, with the bulk of the cordwood stacked to the rear. On the right-hand side the cord lay in disarray on the floor, as if a heap of them had fallen forward.

Deakin's eyes had become very still and watchful. His nose wrinkled and after a few moments his eyes shifted sideways and downwards. Deakin stooped, reached be hind some tangled pieces of cordwood, straightened and held out a bottle.

'Tequila. He was reeking of the stuff, had some of it spilled on his clothes.' He looked incredulously at Banlon. 'And you knew nothing – nothing of this?'

'Just what I was going to ask.' Pearce looked and sounded grim.

'God's my witness, Marshal.' If Banlon kept shrinking at his present rate his eventual disappearance was only a matter of time. 'I've no sense of smell – ask anybody. I didn't know Jackson until he joined us at Ogden – and I never even knew that he drank that stuff.'

'You know now.' Claremont had made his appearance in the cab. 'We all know now. Poor devil. As for you, Banlon, I'm putting you under military law. Any more drinking and you'll end up in a cell in Fort Humboldt and I'll have you dismissed the Union Pacific.'

Banlon tried to look aggrieved but his heart wasn't in it. 'I never drink on duty, sir.'

'You were drinking yesterday afternoon at the Reese City depot.'

'I mean when I'm driving the train –'

'That'll do. No more questions, Marshal?'

'Nothing more to ask, Colonel. It's open and shut to me.'

'Right.' Claremont turned back to Banlon. 'I'll have Bellew detail a trooper as fireman.' He made a gesture of dismissal and made to turn away.

Banlon said hurriedly: 'Two things, Colonel.' Claremont turned. 'You can see we're running low on fuel and there's a depot about a mile and a half up the valley –'

'Yes, yes. I'll detail a loading party. And – ?'

'I'm pretty well bushed, sir. And this business of Jackson . . . If Devlin — that's the brake-man — could relieve me in a couple of hours — '

'That shall be arranged.'

A soldier in a peaked cavalryman's cap peered out from the side of the locomotive through the now heavily falling snow. He said to Banlon: 'I think this must be the fuel dump coming up.'

Banlon joined them, nodded, returned to the controls and brought the train to a gentle stop, so positioning it that it brought up with locomotive and tender precisely opposite the fuel dump, an open-faced, three-sided shack piled high with cordwood. Banlon said: 'Fetch the loading detail, would you?'

The loading detail, about a dozen men in all, were on the scene in only a matter of seconds and a remarkably unhappy band of troopers they appeared to be. One had the impression that, given the option, they'd have taken on twice their number of hostile Indians rather than the chore on hand and their reluctance for the appointed task was wholly understandable: although it was now approaching noon, the sky was so dark and the now wind-whipped snow so heavy that the light was no better than that of late dusk and visibility no more than a few feet; and the cold was deepening with the passing of every moment. The soldiers, shivering with cold and stamping their feet, lined up with their backs to the developing blizzard and passed the cordwood arm to arm between the fuel store and the tender. And they moved very quickly indeed: no one had to tell them that the sooner they had finished, the sooner they were back in the comparative warmth of their coaches.

Some way back on the other side of the train, an indistinct figure moved quickly and silently along the track.

ide and climbed silently on to the platform at the front of the supply wagon. The door was locked. The man, wearing an army overcoat and a peaked cavalryman's cap, stooped, examined the lock, produced a heavy bunch of keys, selected one and inserted it. The door opened at once, and closed almost immediately as the man entered.

A match scratched, flared and a small oil-lamp came to life. Deakin brushed snow from his great-coat – O'Brien had provided him with some protection against the elements – moved towards the centre of the wagon and looked around him.

To the rear of the coach, packed four deep and two wide in obviously makeshift racks on either side of the central aisle, were exactly thirty-two coffins, all of them identical in shape and size : whoever made coffins for the army apparently visualized all cavalrymen as being exactly the same shape, size and weight. Most of the rest of the wagon was given up to supplies of one kind and another. The right-hand side was given up to neatly stored piles of bagged and crated food supplies. All the left-hand side was stacked with brass-bound oiled wooden boxes, which took up a relatively small space, and unidentified objects lashed down under tarpaulins. The wooden boxes bore the legend : MEDICAL CORPS SUPPLIES : UNITED STATES ARMY. Deakin lifted a corner of the first tarpaulin. The boxes there, also oiled wood, bore the marking, in large red letters : DANGER ! DANGER ! DANGER ! The next few tarpaulins covered boxes similarly marked. The last and smallest tarpaulin to be lifted revealed a tall narrow grey box with a leather carrying handle. It was marked : US ARMY POSTS & TELEGRAPHS.

Deakin lifted off the tarpaulin covering this box, rolled , thrust it under his coat, picked up the grey box, doused the lamp and left, locking the door behind him. Even during the brief time he had been inside the supply wagon the visibility had become appreciably worse. It was as well, Deakin reflected, that they had the security of the railway lines to guide them on their way: in such weather, a horse and rider, or horses and coaches, would, like as not, have ended up in the depths of the ravine.

Lugging the heavy transmitter and now making little attempt at concealment, Deakin hurried along the length of the supply wagon and climbed up the front platform of the leading horse wagon. The door was unlocked. He passed inside, closed the door, lowered the transmitter, located and lit an oil-lamp.

Nearly all the horses were standing, the majority of them chewing mournfully on the hay from the mangers bolted to the side of the wagon. They had little enough room to move in their individual stalls but seemed unconcerned about it. Nor did they show much concern for Deakin's presence. Such few as bothered to acknowledge his presence looked at him incuriously, then as idly turned their heads away.

Deakin paid no attention to the horses. He was much more interested in the source of their food supply, a wood-slatted haybox by his right shoulder that reached almost to the roof. He removed the two top slats, climbed on to the top of the hay and burrowed a deep hole at the back, hard against the side of the wagon. He swung down to the floor, wrapped the transmitter in the tarpaulin, carried it to the top of the haybox, buried it deep in the hole and covered it with hay to a depth of almost three feet. Even allowing for the most evil mischance Deakin reckoned, the transmitter should remain undetected for at least twenty-four hours: and twenty-four hours would be all he would ever want.

He doused the lamp, left and made his way to the rear end of the second coach. He shook out his coat on the platform, went inside, hung the coat on a hook in the passageway outside the officers' sleeping cubicles and made his way forward, sniffing appreciatively as he went. He stopped and looked through an open doorway to his right.

The galley was small but spotless with an array of pots simmering gently on the wood-burning stove. The occupant, when he turned, proved to be a short and very plump Negro most incongruously dressed in a regulation galley uniform, complete even to the chef's tall white hat. He smiled widely at Deakin, teeth white and shining and perfect.

'Morning, sir.'

'Good morning. You must be Carlos, the chef?'

'That's right.' Carlos beamed happily. 'And you must be Mr Deakin, the murderer. Just in time for some coffee, sir.'

Claremont by his side, Banlon stood on the footplate of the locomotive, examining the tender. He turned and leaned out.

'That's the lot. Full. Many thanks.'

Sergeant Bellew raised a hand in acknowledgment, turned and said something to his men, who at once trudged thankfully away in the direction of their coaches, being lost to sight almost at once in the whitely swirling gloom.

Claremont said : 'Ready to roll then, Banlon?'

'Just as soon as this snow-squall clears, Colonel.'

'Of course. You said you wanted the brake-man to relieve you. This would be a good time.'

Banlon said very firmly : 'I did say that, but this would

not be a good time, sir. For the next three miles, I want Devlin right where he is.'

'The next three miles?'

'To the top of Hangman's Pass. The steepest climb in all the mountains.'

Claremont nodded. 'A brake-man could have his uses.'

FIVE

Fort Humboldt lay at the head of a narrow and rock-strewn valley which debouched on to a plain to the west. The strategic position of the Fort had been excellently chosen. Behind it, to the north, was a sheer cliff-face: to the east and south it was bounded by a ravine, narrow but very deep, the eastern arm of which was traversed by a trestle railway bridge: the railway line itself passed east-west in front of the Fort descending slowly down the winding valley into the plain beyond. From the point of view of defence Fort Humboldt could not have been more advantageously located. It could be approached only across the bridge or up the valley; facing in either direction, a small group of determined and well-entrenched men could have easily held off ten times their number.

Architecturally, the Fort itself had no claims to originality. Built years before the completion of the Union Pacific Railway in 1869, it had to depend entirely on local building materials, and the plentiful stands of conifers provided unlimited supplies of that. The wooden stockade was built in the customary form of a hollow square with a boardwalk, about four feet from the top of the stakes, running the entire length of the inside perimeter. The heavy gate, facing both railroad and the river which wound down the valley, lay to the south; immediately inside the gate there was, to the right, the guard-house and to the left the store for weapons, ammunition and explosives. The entire eastern side of the compound was given over to stables. To the western side were the troops' quarters and cookhouse; the northern side was given over to officers' quarters, administrative and telegraph offices, sick bay and some spare accommodation for the invariably weary travellers who made Fort Humboldt a port of call with a not surprising frequency; it was a long long way from any other place.

Approaching the Fort from the west – up valley – were a group of weary travellers who were clearly looking forward very keenly to whatever the Fort might offer them in the way of shelter and hospitality. They were Indians, wrapped to the ears in an unavailing attempt to protect themselves from the biting cold and the thinly falling snow. Tired, very tired, they looked, but not as exhausted as their horses, who were literally trudging through the fetlock-deep snow. Of them all, only their leader, an unusually pale-faced and strikingly handsome Indian, seemed unweary. He sat very erect in the saddle. But then, the chief of the Paiutes always did.

He led his men through the open and unguarded doorway, raised his hand in a gesture of dismissal and headed across the compound, bringing up at a wooden hut with, above the door, the legend COMMANDANT. The Indian dismounted, climbed the few steps and entered, closing the door quickly behind him to keep out the swirling snow.

Sepp Calhoun was seated in Colonel Fairchild's desk armchair, his feet on the Colonel's desk, one of the Colonel's cheroots in one hand and a glass of the Colonel's whisky in the other. He looked up, swung his feet to the floor and rose, a most unusual gesture of respect on the part of Sepp Calhoun, who customarily showed no respect towards anyone. But then, people did not show disrespect to this particular Indian. Not twice.

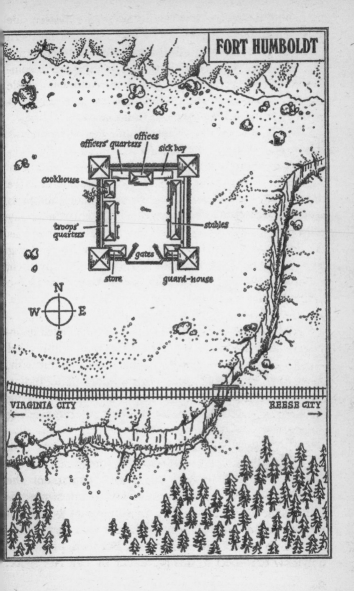

Calhoun said: 'Welcome home, White Hand. You made fast time.'

'In weather such as this the wise man does not linger.'

'All went well? The line to San Francisco –'

'Is cut.' Imperiously, almost contemptuously, White Hand waved away the proffered bottle of whisky. 'We destroyed the bridge over the Anitoba gorge.'

'You have done well, White Hand. You and your men. How much time do we have?'

'Before the soldiers from the west could reach here?'

'Yes. Not that there's any reason to assume that they think that there is anything wrong in Fort Humboldt and will be coming here anyway. But chances we cannot take.'

'The stakes are high, Sepp Calhoun.' He thought briefly. 'Three days. Not less.'

'More than enough. The train arrives tomorrow between noon and sundown.'

'The soldiers on the train – ?'

'No word yet.' Calhoun hesitated, then cleared his throat apologetically. 'It would be as well, White Hand, if you and your braves have some hours of rest. You may need to ride again before dark.'

There was silence during which White Hand regarded a highly uncomfortable Calhoun with total impassivity, then he said: 'There are times, Calhoun, when White Hand questions your judgment. We had an agreement, you remember, about capturing this fort. You and your friends were to come here in the hours of darkness and seek lodging for the night. You would be invited to spend the night, for you are white men and the night was full of snow. So much came true. Then you were to kill the night guards, open the gates, let us in and fall upon the soldiers in their bunks.'

Calhoun reached for his bottle of bourbon.

'It was a wild night, White Hand. We could not see well. The night, as you say, was full of snow and there was a great storm blowing. We thought –'

'The storm was in your minds and the snow came from that bottle of fire-water. I could smell it. So two of the guards they did not kill and there was time for a warning. Not enough time, Calhoun, but enough that fifteen of my best men lie dead. Fire-water! Bourbon! And the white men are better than the red!'

'Now look, White Hand. You must understand –'

'I understand everything. I understand that you care only for yourself, your friends who are all bad men, but not for the Paiutes. Then we ride a night and a day to destroy the Anitoba bridge. This, too, we did. And now you ask us to ride again.'

Calhoun was at his most nervously soothing. 'Only perhaps, White Hand. Those troops *must* be prevented from arriving here. You know that.'

'I may lose more men, it is sure that I will lose more men. I may lose many more men. But not for you, Calhoun, not for your evil bourbon, but for what they have done to my people the army of the white men are my enemies and will be while White Hand lives. But they, too, are brave and skilful fighters. And if they find out that it is White Hand and the Paiutes who have attacked them they will never rest until they have hunted down and destroyed each last one of us. I say the price is too high, Sepp Calhoun.'

'And if there is no white man left to tell what happened?' Calhoun let this thought take hold, then went on softly, persuasively: 'The rewards are even higher.'

After a long pause, White Hand nodded several times. 'The rewards are even higher.'

Fifteen minutes after the troop train had embarked on its laborious crawl up Hangman's Pass, Marica stood gazing through the day compartment window, oblivious both of the six men seated behind her and the icy chill of glass against which her forehead rested. She said to no one in particular : 'What a fantastic view !'

She could hardly be faulted for her comment. The blizzard-like squall had passed away and from where she stood she could see the track curving round and downwards for the space of almost two miles as it followed the breathtaking contours of the conifer-lined white valley until it reached the spidery bridge spanning the gorge at the foot of the valley. As was so often the case after snow had ceased to fall, everything could be seen with preternatural clarity.

Claremont was uninterested in the view; he had more pressing and disturbing matters on his mind. He said : 'Made any progress with your enquiries, Marshal?'

'No, sir.' Pearce wasn't demonstrably unhappy, because it wasn't in his nature either to feel or express such an emotion, but he certainly couldn't have been described as ebullient. 'Nobody knows anything, nobody's seen anything, nobody did anything, nobody heard anything and nobody as much as suspects anybody else. No, sir, you can take it that I haven't made any progress.'

'Oh, I don't know.' Deakin spoke encouragingly. 'Every little elimination helps, doesn't it, Marshal? For instance, I was tied up, so it couldn't have been me. Means you've got only eighty-odd suspects left, Marshal. For a man of –'

Deakin broke off as a sharp report was heard. Claremont, already half out of his seat, said in the voice of a man who knew that impending doom was no longer at hand but had arrived: 'In God's name, what was that?'

Marica must have left him in no doubt as to the accuracy of his diagnosis. Her voice rose to a scream. 'No! No! No!'

Apart from Claremont, Pearce and Deakin there were three other men in the compartment – O'Brien, the Governor and the Rev. Peabody. Within two seconds the last of them had propelled himself to his feet and flung himself towards the nearest window on Marica's side. The faces of the six reflected, or appeared to reflect, all the consternation, shock and horror that Marica's voice had held.

The last three wagons of the train – the two troop-carrying coaches and the brake-van – had broken away from the main body of the train and were already rolling quite quickly back down the long steep descent of Hangman's Pass. The rapidly widening gap between the leading troop coach and the second of the horse-wagons showed just how rapidly the three runaway wagons were accelerating.

Deakin shouted: 'For God's sake, jump! Jump now! Before it's too late.'

But nobody jumped.

The middle wagon of the three runaways – the second troop coach in which Sergeant Bellew was quartered – was already beginning to sway and rattle in the most alarming fashion. The clickety-click of the wheels crossing the expansion joints in the lines increased in tempo with the passing of every moment; and as the fish-plates which held the lines were secured to the sleepers by spikes and not by bolts there was a mounting danger that the track itself might begin to work loose from the bed.

The confusion among the soldiers in the coach was total, their expressions ranging from the dumbfounded to the panic-stricken. Most of the men – all of them struggling to maintain their balance – were milling about wildly without any set purpose or intent, but two pairs of soldiers, lashed by the urgency of Bellew's voice, struggled desperately to open two side doors. After only a few fruitless moments they gave up. One of the soldiers raised his voice above the bedlam of sound.

'Godalmighty!' His voice was only one degree short of a shriek. 'The doors are locked! From the outside!'

In fascinated horror, the six men and the girl in the day compartment, completely without any power to help, continued to watch the runaways, now quarter way round the quarter circle curve of Hangman's Pass and at least a mile distant, remorselessly accelerating and terrifyingly swaying to the extent that wheels were now beginning to lift clear of the track.

Claremont shouted: 'Devlin! The brake-man! Why in God's name doesn't he do something?'

The same thought, though understandably with even more urgency, was in the mind of Sergeant Bellew.

'The brake-man! The brake-man! Why doesn't he do – what in God's name is he doing?'

Bellew ran or more correctly staggered along the wildly shaking and vibrating aisle towards the rear door, a matter made easier by the fact that the central space was clear, nearly all the soldiers having their terrified faces pressed close against the windows, their minds mesmerized by the blurring landscape and hypnotized by shock into the blind acceptance of the inevitable.

Bellew reached the rear door. He tugged desperately and completely without avail at the handle; this door, too, was locked. Bellew drew his Colt and shot above and to the side of the handle. He fired four times, oblivious of two ricochets which whistled with lethal potential through the coach; by this time there were more deadly dangers abroad than ricochets. After the fourth shot the door yielded to the desperate pressure of Bellew's hand.

He emerged on to the rear platform and was almost immediately thrown off by the combination of a wind which had now reached near-hurricane force and an exceptionally violent lurch of the coach. To save himself he had to grab desperately at the rail with both hands. His Colt had been in his right hand : now it went spinning over the side.

Bellew took a suicidal chance, but between sudden death by suicide and sudden death through external causes there lies no difference. He flung himself towards the front platform on the brake van, caught the rail, dragged himself to temporary safety and seized the door of the brake van. This he twisted, pulled and pushed with a close to fear-crazed violence, but this door, by now predictably, was also locked. Bellew flattened his face against the glass panel to the side of the door and peered inside; his eyes widened and his face became masked in the total and final despair of a knowledge that comes too late.

The big brake wheel was at the end of the van but there was no hand on this wheel. Instead, the hand clutched a Bible, which was opened, face down, on the floor of the van. Devlin himself, also face down, lay beside his makeshift bed; between the thin shoulder protruded the hilt of a knife.

Bellew turned his stricken face sideways and stared almost uncomprehendingly, at the snow-laden pine lining the track-side stream whizzing by in a hundred mile-an-hour blur. Bellew crossed himself, something he hadn't done since boyhood, and now the fear was gone from his face. In its place there was only resignation, the acceptance of the inevitability of death.

In the day compartment the seven horrified watchers were without speech for there was no longer anything to say. Like Bellew, although with a vastly different outlook they too had dumbly accepted the inevitability of death.

The runaway coaches, two miles away now and still somehow miraculously remaining on the track, were hurtling towards the final curve leading to the bridge. Marica jerked convulsively away from the window and buried her face in her hands as the runaways failed to negotiate the last bend. They shot off the track – whether they ripped the track off with them or not it was impossible to tell at that distance – toppled sideways as they then sailed out across the void of the gorge, turning over almost lazily in mid-air until the three coaches, still locked together, had assumed a vertical position, a position they still occupied when all three smashed simultaneously into the precipitous far cliff-side of the gorge with the explosive thunderclap of sound of a detonating ammunition dump. Unquestionably, for every man aboard those coaches death must have supervened instantaneously. For a long second of time the flattened, mangled coaches remained in that position, seemingly pinned against the canyon wall as if unwilling to move, then, with a deliberation and slowness in grotesque contrast to their speed at the moment of impact, dropped reluctantly off and tumbled lazily into the unseen depths below.

The eleven survivors of the original trainload from Reese City, most of them shivering violently, were gathered round the rear end of the second horse wagon – now, in effect, the end of the train – examining the coupling, the free end of which had formerly been bolted to the front of the leading troop wagon. Three of the four massive securing bolts were still loosely in place in the plate. Claremont stared unbelievingly at the plate and the bolts.

'But how, how, *how* could it have happened? Look at the size of those bolts!'

O'Brien said: 'Not that I have any intention of going down into that ravine to investigate – even although all the evidence is smashed to pieces anyway – but what *I'd* have liked to see was the condition of the timber to which those bolts were attached.'

'But I thought I heard a report –'

'Or,' Deakin suggested, 'a baulk of heavy timber snapping in half.'

'Of course.' Claremont dropped the chain and plate. 'Of course. That's what it must have been. But *why* should it – Banlon, you're the engineer. In fact, you're the only trainman we have left.'

'Before God, I've no idea. The wood may have rotted – it can happen without showing any signs – and this *is* the steepest climb in the mountains. But I'm only guessing. What *I* can't understand is why Devlin did nothing about it.'

Claremont was sombre in both face and voice. 'Some answers we'll never know. What's past is past. First thing is to have another try to contact Reese City or Ogden – we must have replacements for those poor devils at once, God rest their souls. What a way to die! The only way for a cavalryman to die is in the face of the enemy.' Claremont wasn't quite as pragmatic as he would have liked to sound and he had to make a conscious effort to return himself to the realities of the present. 'At least, thank God, we didn't lose those medical supplies.'

Deakin was clearly in no mood to commiserate with Claremont. 'Wouldn't have made any difference if you had.'

'Meaning?'

'Medical supplies aren't much good without a doctor to administer them.'

Claremont paused for a few seconds. 'You're a doctor.'

'Not any more I'm not.'

They had a close circle of listeners. Even a trace of interest was beginning to show in Marica's still rather shocked face.

Claremont was becoming heated. 'But, damn it all, Deakin, that's cholera they have up there. Your fellow man—'

'My fellow man's going to hang me. Probably, in spite of Pearce's protestations, from the nearest cottonwood tree. The hell with my fellow man. Besides, as you say, that's cholera they've got up there.'

Claremont showed as much contempt as it is possible for a man to do without actually sneering. 'And that's your real reason?'

'I think it's a very good reason.'

Claremont turned away in disgust and looked around the shivering company. 'Morse I've never learnt. Can anyone—'

'I'm no Ferguson,' O'Brien said. 'But if you give me time—'

'Thank you, Major. Henry, you'll find the set in the front of the supply wagon, under a tarpaulin. Bring i through to the day compartment, will you?' He turned to Banlon, his mouth bitter. 'I suppose the only good point about this ghastly business is that we'll be able to make better time to the Fort. With those wagons gone—'

Banlon said heavily: 'We won't make better time. Devlin was the only other person aboard who could drive this train—and I've got to have sleep some time.'

'My God, I'd quite forgotten. Now?'

'I can make twice the speed in the day that I can by night. I'll try to hang on to nightfall. By that time—' he nodded to his fireman soldier standing by—'Rafferty and I are going to be pretty bushed, Colonel.'

'I understand.' He looked at the dangling chain and the plate on the ground. 'And how about the safety factor, Banlon?'

Banlon spent quite some time rubbing the white bristles on his wizened face, then said: 'I can't see it, Colonel. Any problem, that is. Four things. This has been a million to one chance—I've never heard of it before—and it's one to a million that it will happen again. I've got a lot less weight to pull so the strain on the couplings is going to be that much less. This is the steepest gradient on the line and once we're over the top it's going to be that much easier.'

'You said four things. That's three.'

'Sorry, sir.' Banlon rubbed his eyes. 'Tired, that's all. What I'm going to do now is to get a spike and hammer and test the woodwork around each coupling plate. Only sure way to test for rot, Colonel.'

'Thank you, Banlon.' He transferred his attention to the returning Henry who wore upon his face the expression of a man whom fate can touch no more. Ready?'

'No.'

'What do you mean – no?'

'I mean the set's gone.'

'What!'

'It's not in the supply wagon, that's for sure.'

'Impossible.'

Henry stared silently into the middle distance.

'Are you sure?' It wasn't so much disbelief in Clare
mont's tone as a groping lack of understanding, th
wearied bafflement of a man to whom too many incom
prehensible things have happened too quickly.

Henry assumed an air of injured patience which sa
well upon his lugubrious countenance. 'I do not wish t
seem impertinent to the Colonel but I suggest the Colone
goes see for himself.'

Claremont manfully quelled what was clearly an in
cipient attack of apoplexy. 'All of you! Search the train!

'Two things, Colonel,' Deakin said. He looked aroun
and ticked numbers off his fingers. 'First is, of the te
people you're talking to, Rafferty is the only one you ca
order about. None of the rest of us is under your com
mand, directly or indirectly, which makes it a bit awk
ward for martinet colonels accustomed to instant obedi
ence. Second thing is, I don't think you need bothe
searching.'

Claremont did some even more manful quelling, the
finally and silently gave Deakin a coldly interrogativ
look.

Deakin said: 'When we were refuelling this mornin
I saw someone take a case about the size of a transmitte
from the supply wagon and walk back along the trac
with it. The snow was pretty thick and the visibility –
well, we all remember what that was like. I just couldn'
see who it was.'

'Yes? Assuming it was Ferguson, why should he do a thing like that?'

'How should I know? Ferguson or no Ferguson, I didn't speak to this person. Why should I do your thinking for you?'

'You become increasingly impertinent, Deakin.'

'I don't see there's a great deal you can do about that.' Deakin shrugged. 'Maybe he wanted to repair it.'

'And why take it away to do that?'

Deakin showed an uncharacteristic flash of irritation. How the hell should – ' He broke off. 'Is the supply wagon heated?'

'No.'

'And it's way below freezing. If he wanted to carry out some repairs or maintenance he'd take it to a heated place – one of the troop wagons. And they're both at the bottom of that ravine now – including the transmitter. There's your answer.'

Claremont had himself well under control. He said thoughtfully : 'And you're pretty glib with *your* answers, Deakin.'

'Oh my God ! Go and search your damned train, then.'

'No. You're probably right, if only because there would appear to be no other explanations.' He took a step closer to Deakin. 'Something's familiar about your face.' Deakin looked at him briefly then looked away in silence. 'Were you ever in the army, Deakin?'

'No.'

'Union or Confederate, I mean?'

'Neither.'

'Neither?'

'I've told you, I'm not a man of violence.'

'Then where were you in the War between the States?'

Deakin paused as if trying to recall, then finally said : 'California. The goings-on in the east didn't seem all tha important out there.'

Claremont shook his head. 'How you cherish the safety of your own skin, Deakin.'

'A man could cherish worse things in life,' Deakin said indifferently. He turned and walked slowly up the track Henry, his lugubrious eyes very thoughtful, watched him go. He turned to O'Brien and spoke softly :

'I'm like the Colonel. I've seen him before, too.'

'Who is he?'

'I don't know. I can't put a name to him and I can' remember where I saw him. But it'll come back.'

Shortly after noon it had started to snow again but no heavily enough to impair forward visibility from the cab The train, now with only five coaches behind the tender was making fair speed up the winding bed of a valley, a long plume of smoke trailing out behind. In the dining saloon all but one of the surviving passengers were sitting down to a sombre meal. Claremont turned to Henry.

'Tell Mr Peabody that we're eating.' Henry left and Claremont said to the Governor : 'Though God knows I've got no appetite.'

'Nor I, Colonel, nor I.' The Governor's appearance did not belie his words. The anxiety of the previous night was still there but now overlaid with a new-found haggard pallor. The portmanteau bags under his eyes were dark and veined and what little could be seen of the jowls behind the splendid white beard was more pendulous than ever. He was looking less like Buffalo Bill by the minute. He continued : 'What a dreadful journey, what a dreadful journey ! All the troops, all those splendid boys gone. Captain Oakland and Lieutenant Newell missing

– and *they* may be dead for all we know. Then Dr Molyneux – he *is* dead. Not only dead, but murdered. And the Marshal has no idea who – who – My God! He might even be sitting here. The murderer, I mean.'

Pearce said mildly: 'The odds are about ten to one that he isn't, Governor. The odds are ten to one that he's lying back in the ravine there.'

'How do you know?' The Governor shook his head in slow despair. 'How can anyone know? One wonders what in the name of God is going to happen next.'

'I don't know,' Pearce said. 'But judging from the expression on Henry's face, it's happened already.'

Henry, who had that moment returned, had a hunted air about him. His hands were convulsively opening and closing. He said in a husky voice: 'I can't find him, sir. The preacher, I mean. He's not in his sleeping quarters.'

Governor Fairchild gave an audible moan. Both he and Claremont looked at each other with the same dark foreboding mirrored in their eyes. Deakin's face, for a moment, might have been carved from stone, his eyes bleak and cold. Then he relaxed and said easily: 'He can't be far. I was talking to him only fifteen minutes ago.'

Pearce said sourly: 'So I noticed. What about?'

'Trying to save my soul,' Deakin explained. 'Even when I pointed out that murderers have no soul he –'

'Be quiet!' Claremont's voice was almost a shout. 'Search the train!'

'And stop it, sir?'

'Stop it, O'Brien?'

'Things happen aboard this train, Colonel.' O'Brien didn't try to give any special significance to his words, he didn't have to. 'He may be on it. He may not. If he's not, he must be by the track; he can't very well have fallen down a ravine for there have been none for over an hour. If he were to be found outside, then we'd have to reverse down the line and every yard further we go on – '

'Of course. Henry, tell Banlon.'

Henry ran forward while the Governor, Claremont, O'Brien and Pearce moved towards the rear. Deakin remained where he was, evidently with no intention of going anywhere. Marica looked at him with an expression that was far from friendly. The dark eyes were as stony as it was possible for warm dark eyes to be, the lips compressed. When she spoke it was with a quite hostile incredulity.

She said in a tone that befitted her expression: 'He may be sick, injured, dying perhaps. And you just sit there. Aren't you going to help them look for him?'

Deakin leaned back leisurely in his chair, his legs crossed, produced and lit a cheroot. He said in what appeared to be genuine surprise: 'Me? Certainly not. What's he to me? Or I to him? The hell with the Reverend.'

'But he's such a *nice* man.' It was difficult to say whether Marica was more aghast at the impiety or the callous indifference. 'Why, he sat there and talked to you – '

'He invited himself. Now let him look after himself.'

Marica said in disbelief, slowly spacing the words: 'You just don't care.'

'That's it.'

'The Marshal was right and I was wrong. I should have listened to a man of the world. Hanging *is* too good for you. You must be the most self-centred, the most utterly selfish man in the world.'

Deakin said reasonably: 'Well, it's better to be best at

something than best at nothing. Which reminds me of something else that is very good indeed.' He rose. 'The Governor's bourbon. Now seems like an excellent chance to help myself when they're all busy.'

He left along the passageway past the Governor's and Marica's sleeping quarters. Marica remained where she was for a few moments, the anger in her face now with an element of puzzlement in it, hesitated, rose and walked quietly after Deakin. By the time she had reached the door of the officers' day compartment, Deakin had crossed to the cabinet above the sofa at the front end of the coach, poured some bourbon into a tumbler and drained the contents in one savage gulp. Marica watched, her face now showing only wonderment and an increasing lack of comprehension, as Deakin poured himself some more bourbon, drank half of it and turned to the right, gazing with seemingly unseeing eyes through the window. The lean, dark, bitter face was set in lines of an almost frighteningly implacable cruelty.

Eyes widening under a furrowed brow, Marica advanced slowly and silently into the compartment and was less than four feet away from him when Deakin turned, the same almost viciously hard expression on his face. Marica recoiled before it, taking a step back almost as if expecting to be struck. Several seconds elapsed before Deakin appeared to become aware of her presence. His face gradually assumed its normal expression – or lack of it. He said, affably: 'Quite a start you gave me, ma'am.'

She did not answer at once. She advanced like a sleep-walker, her face still full of wonder, lifted a hand and tentatively, almost apprehensively, touched his lapel. She whispered: 'Who are you?'

He shrugged. 'John Deakin.'

'*What* are you?'

'You heard what the Marshal said – '

He broke off as the sound of voices came from the passageway, loud voices that carried with them the connotation of gesticulating hands. Claremont entered, followed by the Governor, Pearce and O'Brien. Claremont was saying : 'If he's not here, he must have fallen off and be lying by the track-side. And he's not here. If we back up, say, five miles – '

Fairchild interrupted, one more vexation added to his sea of troubles. 'Damn you, Deakin. That's my whisky!'

Deakin gave an acknowledging nod. 'And excellent stuff it is, too. You don't have to be afraid of offering this to anyone.'

Without a word and without warning Pearce stepped forward and savagely struck Deakin's right wrist, sending the glass flying.

Marica's reaction was involuntary, as surprising to her as it was to the others. She said in sudden anger : 'What a brave man you are, Marshal – with that big gun hanging by your side.'

With the exception of Deakin, everyone stared at her in astonishment. Pearce looked back towards Deakin, the surprise on his face giving way to contempt, a contempt reflected in his gesture as he pulled the Colt from its holster, threw it on the couch and smiled invitingly at Deakin. Deakin made no response. Pearce swung his left hand and hit Deakin, hard, across the lower face with the back of his clenched fist, a humiliating blow with which to strike any man. Deakin staggered and sat down heavily on the sofa, then, after a few seconds during which the other men averted their faces in shame for lost manhood, rose, dabbed some blood from a split lip and walked across to the other corner of the compartment near the entrance to the passageway where, to the accompaniment of the screeching of brakes, the others brushed by him as they hurried to take up observation positions on the platforms. Marica came slowly after them and stopped in front of Deakin. From her reticule she brought out a flimsy wisp of cambric and patted the cut lip. When she spoke, it was in a very quiet tone.

'Poor man,' she said. 'So little time to live.'

'I'm not dead yet.'

'I didn't mean you. I meant the Marshal.'

She walked down the passageway and entered her sleeping compartment without looking back. Deakin looked after her thoughtfully, then crossed to the liquor cabinet and helped himself to some more bourbon.

While Deakin was lowering the level in the Governor's bottle, Banlon backed the train slowly down the valley. Four men stood at the very end of the train, the rear platform of the second horse wagon, heavily wrapped against the biting cold and the thinly falling snow: Claremont and Pearce studied the track-side to the right, the Governor and O'Brien the side to the left. But as mile succeeded crawling mile there was nothing to be seen. The snow on both sides was virginal, untouched except for the faint dusting of soot from the locomotive's earlier passage; nor was the snow heavy enough to have concealed any recent disturbances in the ankle-deep snow on the ground, far less have covered the body of a man. In short, there was no sign of the Reverend Peabody or any mark made by him had he fallen – or been pushed – from the train.

Claremont straightened and turned at the same instant as O'Brien, on the other side of the platform, did the same. Claremont shook his head slowly and O'Brien nodded in reluctant agreement; the latter turned again, leaned far out over the platform safety rail and waved his arm. Banlon, who had for the past fifteen or twenty minutes been looking towards the rear of the train, gave an acknowledging wave of his arm. The train jolted to a halt, then began to move forward again. Reluctantly, the four men on the rear platform moved away from the safety rails and returned to the comparative warmth of the horse wagon.

As soon as they returned to the day compartment Claremont had assembled there, with the exception of Banlon and his soldier-fireman Rafferty, the only eight remaining survivors of the original trainload. The atmosphere was heavy with suspicion and menace, not unmixed with fear. Every person present appeared to be carefully avoiding the eyes of every other person, with the exception of Deakin, who didn't appear to care where he looked.

Claremont passed a weary hand across his forehead.

'It's impossible. It's just absolutely impossible. We *know* that Peabody is not on the train. We *know* he can't have left the train. And nobody saw him after he left this compartment. A man can't just vanish like that.' Claremont looked round the listeners, but there was no help from there, no reaction except the embarrassed shuffling of the feet of Carlos, the Negro cook, who was clearly embarrassed by the unaccustomed presence of the gentry. Claremont repeated : 'Well, he can't, can he?'

'Can't he?' Fairchild said heavily. 'He's done it, hasn't he?'

Deakin said : 'Well, yes and no.'

Pearce's antagonism flared instantly. 'What do you mean – yes and no? What do *you* know about this disappearance, mister?'

'Nothing. How could I? I was here from the time Peabody left till the time Henry reported his disappearance. Miss Fairchild will vouch for that.'

Pearce made to speak but Claremont lifted a restraining hand and turned to Deakin. 'You have something in mind?'

'I have something in mind. True, we haven't crossed any ravines during the time that Peabody could have disappeared. But we did cross over two small trellis bridges in that stretch. The outside of the train is practically level with the sides of the bridges – and neither of those have guard rails. He could have gone from the train over the edge without leaving a trace.'

O'Brien made no attempt to conceal the disbelief in his voice. 'An interesting theory, Deakin. All you have to explain now is *why* he jumped from –'

'He didn't jump. He was pushed. More likely, someone just picked him up and threw him over the edge. He was, after all, a very little man. A big strong person could have thrown him well clear. I wonder who that person could have been. Not me. I've an alibi. Not Miss Fairchild. She's not a big strong man and, anyway, I'm *her* alibi, although I suppose my testimony is worthless in your eyes. But you're big strong men. All of you. Six big strong men.' He paused and surveyed them severally and leisurely. 'I wonder which one of you it was.'

The Governor didn't splutter but he came close. 'Preposterous! Absolutely preposterous!'

Claremont said icily: 'The man's crazy.'

'I'm only trying to find a theory to fit the known facts,' Deakin said mildly. 'Anyone got a better one?'

From the uneasy silence it was apparent that no one had a better one. Marica said: 'But who on earth would want to – to kill a harmless little man like Mr Peabody?'

'I don't know. Who on earth would do away with a harmless old doctor like Molyneux? Who on earth would want to do away with two – I presume – harmless cavalr officers like Oakland and Newell?'

Pearce's suspicions were immediate and inevitable 'Who said anything's happened to them?'

Deakin regarded him for a long and, it seemed, pitying moment; he appeared bent on making it clear that th strength of his determination not to become involved physically with Pearce was matched only by his total dis regard for the man, an attitude that Pearce was mani festly finding more intolerable by the moment. Deakin said: 'If you believe, after all that's happened, that their disappearance is just the long arm of coincidence, then it's time you turned over your badge to someone who isn't solid bone between the ears. Why, Marshal, you might be the man we want.'

Pearce, his face ugly, stepped forward, his fist swing ing, but Claremont quickly interposed himself between him and Deakin and whatever Claremont lacked it wa certainly not authority.

'That will be quite enough, Marshal. There's been to much violence already.'

'I agree entirely with Colonel Claremont.' Fairchild puffed out his cheeks and spoke weightily in his impres sively gubernatorial manner. 'I think we're being pan icked. We don't *know* that anything of what this – thi felon is suggesting is true. We don't *know* that Molyneux *was* murdered –' Fairchild had a splendid gift for em phasis with a telling pause after each word so emphasized – 'and we've only Deakin's word for that, we've only Deakin's word that he, Deakin, *was* a doctor – and w all know what Deakin's word is worth.'

'You're maligning my character in public, Governor, Deakin said. 'There's a law in the constitution that say you – that's me – can seek redress for such unsubstan tiated imputations. I have six witnesses to the fact that you have slandered me.' Deakin looked around him. 'Mind you I wouldn't say that they are all unbiased.'

'The law! The law!' Fairchild had turned an unbecoming turkey red and the popping bloodshot blue eyes appeared to be in some danger of coming adrift from their moorings. 'A scofflaw like you, a murderer, an arsonist, daring to invoke the sacred constitution of our United States!' He paused, probably because of the awareness that he was operating some little way below his thespian best. 'We don't *know* that Oakland and Newell were murdered. We don't actually *know* that Peabody was the victim of –'

'You're whistling in the dark,' Deakin said contemptuously. He looked at the Governor consideringly. 'Or maybe you don't intend to lock the door of your sleeping compartment tonight.' The Governor failed to take advantage of the long-ensuing pause and Deakin went on: 'Unless, of course, you're in a position to know that you personally have nothing to worry about.'

Fairchild stared at him. 'By God, Deakin, you'll pay for that insinuation.'

Deakin said wearily: 'Hark at who's talking about insinuations. Pay for it? With what? My neck? That's already spoken for. My God, it's wonderful. Here you all are, bent on delivering me up to justice, while one of you a killer with the blood of four men on his hands. Maybe not four men. Maybe eighty-four men.'

'Eighty-four men?' Fairchild exercised the last of his rapidly waning hauteur.

'As you put it yourself, Governor, we don't *know* that the loss of the troop wagons was an accident.' Deakin gazed off into the middle distance, then focused again on the Governor. 'Just as we don't *know* that there is only

one of you eight – even though they are not here, w
cannot exclude Banlon and Rafferty although we mus
of course exclude Miss Fairchild – solely responsible fo
the killings. There may be two or more of you felon
acting in concert, in which case all of you would be
equally guilty in the eyes of the law. My training i
medical jurisprudence. Not that any of you would believ
it.'

With an unhurried ostentation Deakin turned his bac
on the company, leaned his elbows on the brass grab-rai
and peered out into the thickening, snow-laden twilight

SIX

Banlon eased the locomotive to a halt, secured the brake, locked it, removed the heavy key, tiredly wiped his brow with a sweat-rag and turned to Rafferty who was propped up against his side of the cab, his eyes half-closed and swaying with utter weariness.

Banlon said : 'Enough.'

'Enough. I'm dead.'

'Two corpses.' Banlon peered out into the snow-filled darkness of the night and shivered. 'Come on. Let's go see your Colonel.'

The Colonel, at that moment, was sitting as close to the wood-burning stove as it was possible for a man to be. Huddled with him were Governor Fairchild, O'Brien, Pearce and Marica. All of them had glasses of various liquids in their hands. Deakin sat on the floor in a remote corner, his shoulders hunched against the cold; predictably, he had no glass in his hand.

The door leading to the front platform opened and Banlon and Rafferty hurried in, accompanied by a blast of freezing air and a thick swirl of snow, and quickly closed the door. They looked white-faced and exhausted. Banlon yawned mightily, politely covering his mouth with his hand; one does not yawn in the presence of governors and colonels. He yawned again, uncontrollably, and said : 'Well, that's it, then, Colonel. We lie down or we fall down.'

'You've done a fine job, Banlon, a splendid job. I won't forget to report this to your Union Pacific employers. As for you, Rafferty, I'm proud of you.' Claremont considered briefly. 'You can have my bunk, Banlon; Rafferty, you have the Major's.'

'Thank you.' Banlon yawned a third time. 'One thing, Colonel. Somebody's going to have to keep the steam up.'

'Seems a waste of fuel. Can't you just let the fire out and light it again?'

'No way.' The emphatic shake of Banlon's head precluded any argument. 'Relighting would waste another couple of hours and use just as much fuel as it would cost to keep steam up. But that doesn't matter. What matters is that if the fires go out and the water in the condenser tubes freezes – well, Colonel, it's still a mighty long walk to Fort Humboldt.'

Deakin rose stiffly to his feet. 'I'm not much of a walker. I'll go.'

'You?' Pearce had also risen, his face at once suspicious. 'What suddenly makes you so co-operative?'

'I don't feel the slightest bit co-operative; the last thing I want to do is to co-operate with any of you lot. But it's my skin as well as yours – and you all know by now how much I cherish my own skin. Also, Marshal, I have very delicate feelings – I can sense I'm not very popular here. And I'm cold – this is a very draughty spot – while it will be nice and warm in the cab. *And* I'd rather not spend the rest of the night watching the lot of you drinking whisky. *And* I'd feel safer the further I am from you – meaning you, Pearce. *And* I'm the only person who can be trusted to go – or had you forgotten, Marshal, that I'm the only person aboard above suspicion?'

Deakin turned and looked enquiringly at Banlon, who in turn looked at Colonel Claremont. Claremont hesitated, then nodded.

Banlon said : 'Rake the fire-box bed every half-hour

Feed in enough fuel to keep the pressure gauge needle between the blue and the red. If it goes over the red, you'll find the steam release valve beside the gauge.'

Deakin nodded and left. Pearce looked uneasily after him, then turned to Claremont.

'I don't like it. What's to stop him from uncoupling the locomotive and driving off himself? We all know that cofflaw will stop at nothing.'

'This is to stop him, Marshal.' Banlon held out the heavy key. 'I've locked the brake wheel. Like to take charge of it?'

'I would indeed.' Pearce took the key, sat down, relaxed and reached for his glass. O'Brien rose at the same moment, nodded to Banlon and Rafferty.

'I'll show you men where to sleep. Come on.'

The three men left the day compartment and O'Brien led the way towards the after end of the second coach. He showed Banlon into Claremont's compartment, then led Rafferty into his own. He waved a hand and said: 'This suit you?'

While Rafferty looked around in dutiful respect O'Brien swiftly extracted a bottle of whisky from a cupboard and held it out in the passageway where it couldn't be seen. Rafferty said: 'Of course. Thank you very much, sir.'

'Fine. I'll say good night, then.' O'Brien closed the door and retraced his steps until he reached the galley. Without even the courtesy of a knock he entered and closed the door behind him. The galley was a tiny place, not more than six by five, and when the space taken up by the cord-fuelled cooking stove, the cupboards for pots, pans, crockery and food were taken into account, there was barely room for the cook to turn around in, far less swing a cat: but Carlos and Henry, each perched on a tiny stool, did not appear to find the accommodation unduly cramped. As O'Brien entered they looked up, each man wearing his habitual expression, Henry his look of lugubrious near-despair, Carlos his dazzling beam.

O'Brien placed the bottle on the tiny work-table. 'You're going to need this. And the warmest clothes you can find. It's a bitter night out. I'll be back shortly.' He looked round curiously. 'Wouldn't you have a lot more room in your own quarters?'

'Yes, indeed, Mr O'Brien.' Carlos smiled hugely and indicated the stove – it was too hot to touch. 'But we wouldn't have this. Warmest place on the train.'

The second warmest place was unquestionably the loco-motive cab. At that moment it was quite a few degrees colder than it would have been normally because of the heavy gusts of driving snow that swirled almost continuously into it; but the fierce red glow from the opened fire-box, which rendered the two oil-lamps momentarily superfluous, at least gave the illusion of warmth. But Deakin, unquestionably, was feeling no cold at all; sweat glistened on his face as he stoked the fire-box.

He fed in a final baulk of cordwood, straightened and glanced at the steam-gauge. The needle was close to the red mark. He nodded to himself in satisfaction and closed the fire-box door. The illumination in the cab was suddenly much reduced and still further so when Deakin unhooked one of the lamps and took it with him into the tender, which was still about two-thirds full of cordwood. He set the lamp on the floor and began to work almost feverishly, transferring the wood from the right to the left side of the tender.

Fifteen minutes later his face no longer glistened with sweat; it was copiously covered with it and this despite the fact that the temperature in the fully exposed tender must have been close on freezing point. But then, shifting heavy baulks of timber at high speed is no light work and Deakin had already transferred at least half of the remaining contents of the tender from the right to the left. He straightened wearily, rubbed an obviously aching back, turned away, moved into the cab and examined the steam-gauge. The needle, during his exertions, had fallen below the blue line. Hurriedly, Deakin opened the fire-box door, raked through the bed, threw some more cordwood into the hungry heart of the fire-box, closed the door and, without even glancing at the steam-gauge, returned to his back-breaking task in the tender.

He had removed no more than twenty baulks when he stopped work abruptly and brought the oil-lamp to examine the remaining pile of cordwood more closely. He set the oil-lamp to one side and threw the next dozen baulks to the left before reaching for the lamp again. He sank slowly to his knees, the normal lack of expression on his face replaced by a hard and bitter anger.

The two men lying huddled together were unmistakably dead, literally frozen stiff. Deakin had removed sufficient cordwood to reveal their upper bodies and faces. Both men had ghastly head wounds, both men wore the uniforms of officers of the United States Cavalry, one a Captain, the other a Lieutenant. Beyond a doubt Claremont's two missing officers, Oakland and Newell.

The anger had left Deakin's face : for a man who lived the life he did, anger, he had long discovered, was an emotion he couldn't afford. He stood and swiftly began to replace the cordwood, stacking it in the neat precise form in which he had found it until it had all been returned to its original position. Understandably, because of this necessity for precision and because of his rapidly increasing tiredness which was now but one stage removed from exhaustion, it took him twice as long to restack the pile as it had taken him to dismantle it.

Finished, he again checked the steam-gauge to find that the needle had now fallen well below the blue line, then again opened the fire-box door to reveal a red glow inside which was now very dull indeed. Wearily, Deakin resumed the stoking and thrust into the box every last baulk of timber it would accommodate. Again he closed the door, again he did not examine the gauge. He pulled his collar high, his hat low and swung down on the track-side into the icy breath-catching driving whiteness of what was now a near-blizzard.

Not bothering too much to conceal his presence – the visibility was now as close to zero as made no difference – Deakin walked back along the track-side, passing first the day-cum-dining coach, then the coach containing the galley and officers' night quarters. As he reached the end of this he stopped abruptly and cocked his head. He could distinctly hear a peculiar glug-glugging sound – peculiar in those circumstances but readily identifiable in more normal circumstances. Deakin eased forward in ghostlike silence and hitched a wary eye round the rear corner of the second coach.

On the leading platform of the third coach – the supply wagon – a man was sitting on the rail, his head tilted back as he drank deeply from the neck of a bottle. Because of the now almost horizontally driving snow and the fact that it was blowing directly from the front to the back of the train, the man was sitting in an almost completely snow-sheltered oasis; Deakin had no difficulty at all in recognizing the man as Henry.

Deakin pressed back against the coach, drew a deep breath of relief, pulled his sleeve across his forehead in another gesture of relief, silently retraced his steps for several paces, then moved directly out from the train and came curving back in a semicircle which took him to a point just to the rear of the supply wagon. This time his approach was a great deal more cautious. He dropped to his hands and knees, crawled cautiously forward and glanced upward. A second man was on guard at the rear of the supply wagon; there was no mistaking the black moonface of Carlos even although the gleaming smile was in noticeable and understandable abeyance.

Deakin repeated the circling tactic and brought up at the rear end of the first horse wagon. He mounted the platform, effected a prudently stealthy entrance and closed the door behind him. As he moved towards the front of the wagon a horse whinnied nervously. Deakin immediately moved towards the horse, stroked its neck and murmured reassuring words; the horse nuzzled his face and fell quiet. If Carlos had heard the sound he paid no attention; apart from the fact that it was a sound that one would naturally expect to hear from a horse wagon, it wasn't much of a night for paying attention.

Arrived at the front end of the wagon, Deakin peered through a crack in the door. Carlos, only a few feet away, appeared to be gloomily contemplating what must have been his very chilly feet indeed. Deakin turned away to the slatted haybox to his left. With great care and in complete silence he removed a few of the top bars and an armful of hay, recovered the telegraph transmitter, replaced the hay and the bars as he had found them, and moved off with the transmitter to the rear of the wagon where he descended the steps, looked quickly to the front and the rear – visibility was still almost nil – stepped down silently into the snow and made his way quickly towards the rear of the train.

A convenient fifty yards from the rear of the train Deakin located a telegraph-pole. He unwound the trailing lead from the transmitter and secured one end to his belt. Then he began to climb the telegraph-pole.

'Began' was the operative word. He managed to get about three feet off the ground, then helplessly remained there, unable to make another inch. The effects of snow, high winds and freezing temperatures had combined to encase the pole in an impenetrable sheath of ice which offered a zero friction coefficient, an entire lack of grip which rendered further progress quite impossible. Deakin returned to earth, stood there for a moment in thought, then tore a quantity of material from his shirt and ripped it into two pieces.

He made for the nearest angled guy wire, wrapped his legs around it, and, using them and the two improvised gloves from his shirt to afford a friction grip, started to climb again. It was a fairly difficult climb and, in the light of what he had recently been through, a most exhausting one, but by no means impossible; by the time he'd reached the top and straddled the crossbar the matter that concerned him most was that his frozen hands felt as if they no longer belonged to him. At that moment frostbite was the very last thing he wanted.

Two minutes of rubbing and kneading his hands and the pain that steadily accompanied this as the circulation returned convinced him that this misfortune had not indeed befallen him. He detached the end of the trailing lead from his belt, secured it firmly to a telegraph wire and returned to earth the way he had come and so swiftly that by the time he arrived there the hands that had so lately felt frozen now felt as if they had been badly burned. He uncovered the transmitter set and bent over it, shielding it as best he could from the snow, and began to transmit.

At Fort Humboldt, where the weather was no better and no worse than it was where Deakin was crouched, Sepp Calhoun, White Hand and two other white men were sitting in the commandant's office. Calhoun, as usual, was using his boots to make free of Colonel Fairchild's desk, while both hands were occupied in similarly making free of the Colonel's whisky and cigars. White Hand was sitting erect in a hard-backed chair, carefully not touching the glass before him. The door opened and a man entered, his face conveying as high a degree of urgency as is possible for one whose bewhiskered and bearded face is liberally covered in snow.

Calhoun and White Hand looked at each other, then moved swiftly towards the door. Even as they reached the telegraph office Carter was transcribing a message. Calhoun glanced briefly at him and Simpson, the other captive telegraph operator, nodded briefly at the two guards and took up his customary position behind the desk. White Hand remained standing. Carter ceased writing and handed a slip of paper to Calhoun, whose face immediately assumed a thunderous expression of frustrated anger.

'Damn it! Damn it! Damn it!'

White Hand said in a quiet voice: 'Trouble, Sepp Calhoun? Trouble for White Hand?'

'Trouble for White Hand. Listen. "Attempt on troop wagons failed. Heavy armed guard on all coaches. Advise." How in God's name did the damned idiots not – '

'Such talk will not help, Calhoun.' Calhoun looked at

him without expression. 'My men and I will help.'

'It's a bad night.' Calhoun went to the door, opened i
and passed outside. White Hand followed, closing th
door behind him. Within moments the figures of the tw
men whitened in the heavy driving snow.

Calhoun said : 'A very bad night, White Hand.'

'The rewards are great. Your words, Sepp Calhoun

'You can do it? Even on a night like this?' Whit
Hand nodded. 'Very well. The entrance to Breakheal
Pass. A cliff on one side, steep slope with plenty of roc
cover for you and your men on the other. You can leav
your horses half a mile – '

'White Hand knows what to do.'

'Sorry. Come on. Let's tell them to instruct Banlon t
stop the train there. You'll never have an easier job
White Hand.'

'I know, I do not like it. I am a warrior and I live t
fight. But massacre I do not like.'

'The rewards are great.'

White Hand nodded in silence. Both men re-entere
the telegraph room where Carter was tapping out
message. Calhoun waved him into stillness, sat at hi
purloined desk, wrote a brief message, handed it to on
of the guards to give to Carter and said to Simpson
'Listen good, friend.'

Carter sent out the communication while Simpso
wrote. At the end of the transmission Calhoun said
'Well, Simpson?'

' "Instruct Banlon halt train two hundred yards insid
east entrance to Breakheart Pass." '

Calhoun nodded approvingly towards Carter. 'Yo
may yet live to be an old man.' As he finished speakin
another message in Morse came in over the headphones
It was very brief and Carter read it out without waitin

'or the usual confirmation from Simpson.

'Affirmative. Signing off.'

Calhoun smiled in as benign a fashion as he was capable of and said : 'We have them, White Hand.'

Judging from the barely perceptible expression on his face, Deakin was not quite of the same opinion. He removed his headphones, with a strong tug pulled the telegraph lead clear from overhead, then gave the telegraph set a shove which sent it tumbling down a steep slope to vanish in the darkness below. He walked away quickly, gave the train a wide berth, arrived at the cab's footplate, brushed the snow from his face, then peered at the steam-gauge.

The needle had fallen dangerously below the blue line. Deakin opened the fire-box, looked at the very dully glowing embers and began to feed cordwood into the fire-box. This time, either through tiredness or concern, he seemed to be in no hurry to go. Instead, he watched the gauge in an almost proprietorial fashion and waited patiently until the needle had climbed up from below the blue line to fractionally above the red one. Banlon had intimated that this was the danger area, but Deakin didn't seem to care. He closed the door on the now fiercely-burning fire-box, took an oil-can and two railroad spikes from Banlon's tool-box, turned up his sheepskin collar and dropped down to the track-side.

He made his by now advisedly circuitous route towards the rear of the train and fetched up stealthily in the close proximity of the rear platform of the supply wagon. Carlos was there, a huddled and shivering Carlos, vainly endeavouring to combat the rigours of the night with the assistance of a bottle of bourbon. Deakin nodded to himself, as if in satisfaction, dropped silently to his hands and knees, crawled under the side of the coach and on to the middle of the track, lowered himself on to his elbows and made his stealthy and extremely slow way along the ties between the rear bogies of the coach. He finally stopped and twisted round with infinite care until he was looking upwards.

Immediately above him was the screwed coupling attaching the rear of the supply wagon to the front of the first horse wagon. Above that again could be seen the rear platform of the supply wagon and the front platform of the horse wagon. On the former and no more than five feet away from Deakin was the clearly observable figure of Carlos.

Very cautiously, so as to avoid any metallic clanking, Deakin gripped the two coupled central links and tried to unscrew them. He desisted almost at once, partly because the task was clearly impossible, partly because of the realization that if he persisted in his effort he was going to leave much of the skin of his palms attached to the frozen metal when the time came for removing his hands. He lifted his oil-can and squirted a generous amount of lubricant on to the screw threads. He heard a sound, lowered the can gently to the snow and turned round very very slowly indeed until he was once more looking upwards.

The sound he had heard was clearly that of Carlos placing his bottle down, for he had just straightened and then started to clump to and fro on the metal platform, stamping his feet and beating his arms, in an attempt to restore circulation. After a few moments he opted for the certainty of internal warmth as opposed to the manifest uncertainty of external warmth and returned to his bottle of bourbon.

Deakin returned to the task on hand. Again he seized

the links, again he twisted and again the result was the same. Nothing. With delicate care he released his grip, fished inside his coat and brought out the two railroad spikes; compared to the coupling links, the metal he now held in his hands felt almost warm. Slowly and carefully he inserted the spikes into the links and twisted again. This time the extra leverage did what was required and the screw turned a fraction, making a slight squeaking noise. Deakin remained absolutely still, then looked slowly upwards. Carlos stirred, straightened from the rail, looked around unenthusiastically, then went back into a huddle with his bottle of bourbon.

Once again Deakin resumed his assault on the bottle screw. Using alternately the oil-can and spikes, he reached, in very short order indeed, the stage where there were not more than two or three threads left. He withdrew the spikes and made the last couple of turns by hand. The two halves of the bottle screw came apart and he lowered them, slowly and in complete silence, until they were dangling vertically at the foot of their respective chains.

Deakin looked up. Carlos hadn't moved. On elbows and knees again Deakin inched back the way he had come, crawled out on to the track-side and made his circumspect way back to the locomotive cab. The needle of the steam-gauge was, predictably, on the blue mark. Some little time later, after another stint of feeding the insatiable maw of the fire-box, an operation that Deakin clearly found to be increasingly distasteful, the needle stood on the red once more. Deakin sank wearily on to a bucket seat in the corner and closed his eyes.

Whether he was asleep or not was impossible to say, but if he were he must have set some sort of timing mechanism in his brain for at fairly regular intervals he started awake, fed some more fuel into the box, then returned to his seat. When Banlon and Rafferty, accompanied by O'Brien, returned to the footplate, they found him hunched on the bucket seat, his head bent, his chin sunk on his chest. He appeared to be asleep. Suddenly he started and looked upwards.

'No more than I expected.' O'Brien's voice was coldly contemptuous. 'Sleeping on the job, eh, Deakin?'

Deakin said nothing, merely pointed a thumb in the direction of the steam-gauge. Banlon crossed and examined it.

'Pretty short sleep, I'd say, Major. Pressure's right up.' He turned round unconcernedly and glanced at the tender; the cordwood was neatly stacked with no signs of having been disarranged. 'And just the right amount of fuel gone, I'd say. A fair enough job. Of course, with all the experience he's had of fires, such as burning down Lake's Crossing – '

'That'll do, Banlon.' O'Brien jerked his head. 'Come on, you.'

Deakin rose stiffly and glanced at his watch. 'Midnight! Seven hours I've been here. You said four.'

'Banlon needed it. What do you want, Deakin? Sympathy?'

'Food.'

'Carlos has made supper.' Deakin privately wondered how Carlos had found time to make supper. 'In the galley. We've eaten.'

'I'll bet you have.'

O'Brien and Deakin descended to the track-side and made their way to the front platform of the leading coach. O'Brien leant far out and waved a hand. Banlon waved an acknowledging hand and disappeared inside the cab. O'Brien turned away and opened the door to the officers' day compartment.

'Coming, then?'

Deakin rubbed his brow. 'In a moment. Don't forget that when the train is stopped no fresh air gets into that cab. After seven hours there I've got a head like a pumpkin.'

O'Brien regarded Deakin for a speculative moment, then obviously and rightly concluding that Deakin could do no mischief standing where he was, nodded and passed inside, closing the door behind him.

Banlon opened up the throttle. The wheels spun on the icy rails, the laboured puffing of the locomotive increased as clouds of smoke belched from the high stack, the puffing slowed abruptly as the wheels bit and the train slowly got under way. With his hand on the grab-rail Deakin leaned far outwards and looked backwards. It was difficult to be certain in the snow-filled darkness, it could have been as much imagination as anything else, but it seemed to him that there was a slight gap opening up between the supply wagon and the first of the horse wagons. A half-minute later, with the train now rounding a gentle curve and so making rearward observation that much easier, Deakin knew for sure that his imagination was not at work. Rapidly fading ghostly blurs in the darkness, the two horse wagons, now at two or three hundred yards' distance, were stationary on the track.

Deakin straightened. Although his face might have appeared at first glance to be its normal, still, inscrutable self, it was perhaps just possible to detect a slight expression of satisfaction. He turned the handle of the door and passed inside. The Governor, Claremont, Pearce and O'Brien were sitting close to the stove, glasses in hand, while Marica, somewhat apart and glassless, sat with her hands demurely folded in her lap. They all looked up at the same moment. O'Brien jerked a thumb in the direction of the rear of the train.

'Food's in the galley.'

'Where do I sleep tonight?'

'You could learn to say "thanks".'

'I can't recall anyone saying "thanks" to me for the seven hours I spent out in that damned cab. Where do I sleep tonight?'

Claremont said: 'Here. Bunk down on one of the couches.'

'What? Next the liquor cabinet?' He made to move away but Claremont's voice stopped him.

'Deakin.' Deakin turned. 'You'd a long haul out there. I didn't mean it that way. Cold?'

'I survived.'

Claremont looked at Governor Fairchild, who hesitated, then nodded. Claremont reached into the cabinet behind him, lifted out a bottle of bourbon and handed it to Deakin, who almost reluctantly accepted it. The Colonel said: 'As Miss Fairchild said, you're innocent until you are proved guilty. If you follow me. Might warm you up a little, Deakin.'

'Thank you, Colonel. I appreciate that.'

Deakin left. As he moved towards the passageway leading to the rear of the coach Marica looked up, the tentative beginnings of a smile on her lips. Deakin walked impassively by and Marica's face became as expressionless as his own.

Almost impossibly, the three of them managed to squeeze into that tiny galley. Carlos and Henry accepted generous measures from Deakin's bottle while Deakin himself set about attacking a meal imposing in quantity but indeterminate in quality: Carlos, understandably, had not been at his culinary best. Deakin scraped the plate with his fork, picked up his own glass and drained it.

Carlos said apologetically: 'Sorry, Mr Deakin, sir. Afraid it got a bit tough in the oven.'

Deakin didn't ask what 'it' was. 'It was fine, just fine and just what I needed.' He yawned. 'And I know what I need now.' He picked up the bourbon bottle, then set it down again. 'Never was much of a drinking man. Think you boys can attend to this for me?'

Carlos beamed 'We'll try, Mr Deakin. We'll certainly try.'

Deakin left for the day compartment. As he entered, the Governor, Claremont, O'Brien and Pearce — Marica was already gone — were leaving for their sleeping quarters, none of them so much as looking at Deakin, far less vouchsafing a word. Deakin, in turn, ignored them. He put some more wood in the stove, stretched out on the settee at the front of the coach, pulled out his watch and looked at it. It was one o'clock.

SEVEN

'One o'clock,' Sepp Calhoun said. 'You will be back by dawn?'

'I shall be back by dawn.' White Hand descended the steps of the commandant's office and joined his men, a least fifty Indians already assembled in the Fort com pound. All were mounted and horses and men were whitely covered in the thickly driving snow. White Hand swung into his own saddle and lifted his hand in grave salute; Calhoun lifted his own in acknowledgment. White Hand wheeled his horse and urged it at a fast cante towards the compound gate; his fifty horsemen followed

Deakin stirred, woke, swung his legs over the edge of the couch and again consulted his watch. It was four o'clock He rose and moved quietly down the passageway pas the Governor's and Marica's sleeping quarters, through the dining compartment and through the end door, ou on to the rear platform of the first coach. From that he transferred to the front platform of the second coach Moving very stealthily now, he peered through th window of the door leading into the second coach.

Not five feet away a pair of lanky legs protruded from the galley out into the passageway. The legs were un mistakably those of Henry. Even as Deakin watched, th legs uncrossed and recrossed themselves. Henry was un mistakably awake.

Deakin drew back from the window, his face thought ful. He moved to one side of the platform, climbed up o

he platform rail, reached up and, after a struggle, succeeded in hauling himself on to the roof. On his hands
and knees, moving from the safety of one central ventilator to the next, he made his way across the precarious
route offered by the snow- and ice-encrusted roof, a
journey made no easier by the jolting, swaying coach.

The train was moving along the side of a narrow and
deep ravine, the track-side closely bordered by heavily
snow-weighted conifers. The sagging branches of the
pines appeared almost to brush the roof of the train. On
two occasions, as if warned by instinct, he glanced over
his shoulder just in time to see such heavy branches
sweeping towards him and both times he had to drop
flat to escape being swept from the roof of the train.

He reached the rear of the second coach, edged his
way forward with millimetric stealth and peered down.
To his total lack of surprise, Carlos, muffled to the ears
against the bitter cold, paced to and fro on the platform.
Deakin inched his way back from the rear edge, turned,
got to his hands and knees and crawled back for a few
feet. Then he stood and continued walking forward,
maintaining his balance only with the greatest difficulty.

The large bough of a pine tree came sweeping towards
him. Deakin didn't hesitate. He knew that if he didn't
do it now it was questionable if he would ever summon
the suicidal resolution to try again. He took a few swift
running backward steps to break the impact of the
branch as it caught him, arms outstretched further to
break the impact, chest-high.

He seized the branch with both hands and realized to
his immediate dismay that it was nowhere near as stout
as he had thought – he had been deceived by its thick
covering of snow. The bough bent. Desperately he swung
his feet up but even at that his back was barely two feet

clear of the roof. He glanced down. An oblivious Carlo‸
pacing to and fro, was momentarily only feet below him
then lost to sight.

Deakin swung his legs down and, facing rearward, hi‸
heels gouging twin tracks in the frozen snow, abruptl‸
released his grip in the knowledge that he had an eve‸
chance of being disembowelled by one of the row c‸
central ventilators.

He was not so disembowelled, but for that fleetin‸
second he was probably unaware of his good fortune, fo‸
though he had made sure to keep his head high the im‸
pact of his back striking against the coach roof was almos‸
literally stunning. Paradoxically enough, it was tha‸
treacherous snow-frosted roof that saved his life. Ha‸
he landed on a dry roof the deceleration factor woul‸
have been so great that he would certainly have lost con‸
sciousness, if not been gravely injured : in either even‸
the result would have been the same – his senseless o‸
broken body would have gone over the edge. As it wa‸
the deceleration factor was minimized by the fact tha‸
his body at once started sliding along the roof – and slid‸
ing at such speed that it seemed not only probable bu‸
certain that he would go shooting out over the rear edg‸
and on to the track below, when damage of a very per‸
manent nature would likely occur to him.

Again, paradoxically, it was the potentially lethal venti‸
lators that were his saving. More by instinct than by cal‸
culated thought he reached out for the first ventilato‸
that came sweeping by. He had the distinct impressio‸
of his right shoulder being wrenched off and his grip wa‸
ruthlessly broken; but it perceptibly slowed his rate c‸
travel. He reached for the next ventilator coming up an‸
the same agonizing process was repeated; but he wa‸
sliding now at hardly more than walking pace. The thir‸

and, he could see, the last ventilator came up. Again he hooked his right elbow round it but this time brought over his left arm and clasped it round his right wrist. He must have grown a new right shoulder for it felt as if this one, too, was coming off. But he held on. His body pivoted through three-quarters of a circle until his legs as far as the knees were protruding over the left-hand side of the roof. But he held on. He knew he had to move then, knew he couldn't hang on much longer. Slowly and in great pain he hauled himself back to the centre line of the coach roof, moved to the rear end and fell rather than lowered himself to the rear platform below.

Gasping for breath, doubled up and totally winded, he sat there for what must have been all of five minutes, feeling like the first man who had gone over Niagara Falls in a barrel. He assessed his injuries: a collection of broken ribs in front where the branch had caught his chest, a similar amount at the back where he'd crashed on to the roof and a shoulder broken in an indeterminate number of places. It took a considerable amount of gingerly investigation to establish that in fact his skeletal system was still intact. Bruising, probably massive bruising there would be and a considerable amount of pain for some time to come, but those he could try both to ignore and forget. They would not incapacitate him. He pulled himself to his feet, opened the rear door of the supply wagon and passed inside.

He moved forward through the banked tiers of coffins and medical supply crates until he came to the front of the supply wagon, where he peered through one of the two small circular observation ports. Carlos was as he had been, pacing to and fro and clearly unaware that anything was amiss. Deakin shook off his sheepskin jacket, fixed it over one of the observation windows and put a piece of heavy sacking over the other. He then lit one of the oil-lamps which hung at intervals along the central length of the coach. Deakin noted with some concern that there was a very narrow chink between two of the planks on the right-hand side and it was barely possible that a thin line of light might show through. But then to observe such a light, if light there was, one would have to be standing to the right of the coach and Carlos was at the front. Besides, there was nothing he could do about it anyway. Deakin dismissed the matter from his mind and turned to the task on hand.

With the aid of a screwdriver and cold chisel with which he had thoughtfully provided himself from Banlon's tool-box, Deakin prised open the lid of a yellow brass-bound oiled wooden box marked MEDICAL CORPS SUPPLIES : UNITED STATES ARMY. The lid came clear with a wrenching, splintering sound but Deakin paid no attention. Nefarious pursuits came much easier on a moving train than on a halted one. The combination of an elderly train, rusted wheels and ancient bogies made sufficient noise as it rattled along the track to preclude normal conversation at a distance of even a few feet. Any noise from within the supply wagon, short of something like a pistol shot, would have been quite inaudible to Carlos, who was in any event concentrating upon other matters. As on an earlier occasion, Carlos had stopped pacing and was relying heavily on liquid internal warmth.

The medical supplies were packed in unusual grey metal containers, unmarked. Deakin picked up one of the tins and opened the lid. The box was packed with gleaming metal shells. Deakin showed no reaction. The discovery, clearly, came as no shock. He opened another two tins. The contents were as before.

Deakin left the wooden crate with its lid wrenched off

– he had apparently passed the point of no return and seemed indifferent as to whether his handiwork was discovered or not – and moved on to another box, the lid of which he levered open with the same disregard for what purported to be US Government property. The contents were as they had been in the previous box. Deakin left and moved towards the rear of the supply wagon, lamp in hand, ignoring all the other wooden boxes marked as containing medical supplies. He reached the stacked tiers of coffins and began to haul one out from the bottom rack. For a supposedly empty coffin, even allowing for the state of his back and shoulder, this manœuvre seemed to cost him a quite disproportionate deal of effort.

Carlos wasn't indulging in anything like so considerable an amount of energy It was apparent that he had not yet lost faith in the efficacy of bourbon as a means of warding off the intense cold; he had the neck of a bottle to his mouth, its base pointing vertically skywards. He lowered the bottle reluctantly, shook and inverted it, all to no purpose. The bottle was empty. Sorrowfully and perhaps a thought unsteadily, Carlos made for the side rail of the platform, leaned out and hurled the bottle into the night. His eyes wistfully followed the flight of the bottle until it disappeared almost immediately into the darkness and the swirling snow. Suddenly the wistful expression vanished, to be replaced not by his normal cheerful beaming expression but by a hard and chilling expression, the suddenly narrowed eyes incongruous in the moonlike face. He momentarily screwed shut those eyes and looked again but what he had seen was still there – a distinct line of light running along the side of the supply wagon. Moving with a speed and delicacy that one would not normally associate with so heavily built a character, he swung across from the rear platform of the second coach to the front platform of the supply wagon. He paused, reached inside his coat and brought out a very unpleasant-looking throwing knife.

At the far end of the wagon Deakin removed a rather sadly splintered lid from the coffin. He lifted the lantern and looked down. His face hardened into bitterness but registered neither surprise nor shock. Deakin had found no more than he had expected to find. The Reverend Peabody's resting-place was not incongruous. He had been dead for many hours.

Deakin loosely replaced the splintered coffin lid and dragged another coffin from its rack on to the wagon floor. From the time taken and the great degree of energy expended, this coffin was obviously very much heavier than the previous one. Deakin used the cold chisel ruthlessly and had the lid off in seconds. He looked down into the interior of the coffin, then nodded almost imperceptibly in far from slow comprehension. The coffin was full to the top with heavily-oiled Winchester repeater rifles, lever action, with tubular magazines on the forestocks.

Deakin threw the lid loosely on top of the coffin, placed the oil-lamp on it, hauled a third coffin to the floor and, with the expertise born of practice, had the lid off in seconds. He had just time to notice that this, too, was full of brand new Winchesters when something caught his sleepless attention and his eyes shifted fractionally to the left. The oil-lamp had flickered, just once, as if in some sudden draught in a place where there shouldn't have been a draught.

Deakin whirled round as Carlos, knife hand already swinging, flung himself upon him. Deakin caught the knife wrist and there was a brief but fierce struggle which ended, temporarily, when both men tripped over a coffin and broke apart in their fall, Deakin falling in an aisle between two rows of coffins, Carlos in the middle of the wagon. Both men were quickly on their feet, although Deakin, despite his aches and pains, or perhaps because of the cold appreciation of the fact that he was the one without a knife, was fractionally the faster. Carlos had changed his grip on his knife and now held it in a throwing position. Deakin, with no room to manœuvre or take evasive action in those narrow confines, kicked savagely at the loose lid of the nearest coffin, the one on which the oil-lamp stood. The lid shot up in the air, momentarily obscuring Deakin from Carlos's view as the lamp shattered on the floor, plunging the supply wagon into comparative darkness. Deakin was in no mood to wait around. To fight in the darkness a man carrying a knife you cannot see is a certain form of suicide.

He ran for the rear door of the supply wagon, went through and closed the door behind him. He didn't even bother looking around him, there was no place to go except up. He scrambled to the roof via the safety rail, stretched himself out and looked down, waiting for Carlos to appear so that he could either jump him or, better, slide back when he did appear, wait for the appearance of his head over the top and kick it off. But the seconds passed and Carlos did not appear. Realization came to Deakin almost too late. He twisted his head around and peered forward into an opaque world filled with greyly driving snow. He rubbed the snow from his eyes, cupped his hand over them and peered again.

Carlos, less than ten feet away, was crawling cautiously along the centre of the roof, knife in one hand and teeth gleaming in a smile in the dark face. Carlos gave the marked impression of one who who was not only enjoying himself but expected to be enjoying himself considerably more in a matter of a second or two. Deakin did not share his feelings, this was one thing he could well have done without; the way he felt at that moment, a robust five-year-old could have coped with him without too much difficulty. There was, in fact, one consideration that slightly lessened the odds against Deakin. Though Carlos's physical faculties seemed quite unimpaired, it was very questionable if the same could be said for his mental ones: Carlos was awash in a very considerable amount of bourbon.

Deakin, on hands and knees now, swung round to face the oncoming Carlos. As he did so, he caught a fleeting glimpse ahead of what seemed, through the snow, to be the beginnings of a long trellis bridge spanning a ravine, but it could have been as much imagined as seen. He had no time for any more. Carlos, now less than six feet away and still with the same gleaming smile of wolfish satisfaction, lifted his throwing hand over his shoulder. He did not look like a man who was in the habit of missing. Deakin jerked his own right hand convulsively forward and the handful of frozen snow it held struck Carlos in the eyes. Blindly, instinctively, Carlos completed his knife throw but Deakin had already flung himself forward in a headlong dive which took him below the trajectory of the knife, his right shoulder socketing solidly into Carlos's chest.

It became immediately apparent that Carlos was not just the big fat man he appeared to be but a big and very powerful man. He took the full impact of Deakin's dive without a grunt – admittedly the icy surface had robbed Deakin of all but a fraction of his potential take-off thrust – closed both hands around Deakin's neck and began to squeeze.

Deakin tried to break the Negro's grip but this proved to be impossible. Savagely, Deakin struck him with all his power – or what was left of it – on both face and body. Carlos merely smiled widely. Slowly, his legs quivering under the strain, Deakin got both feet beneath him and forced himself to a standing position, Carlos rising with him. Carlos, in fact, made no great effort to prevent Deakin from rising, his sole interest was concerned in maintaining and intensifying his grip.

As the two men struggled, fighting in grotesquely slow motion as they tried to maintain their footholds on the treacherous surface, Carlos glanced briefly to his left. Directly below was the beginning of a curving trellis bridge and, below that again, the seemingly bottomless depths of a ravine. His teeth bared, half in savage intensity of effort, half in knowledge of impending triumph as he hooked his fingers ever more deeply into Deakin's neck. It was a measure of his over-confidence, or more likely of the quantity of alcohol inside him, that he apparently quite failed to realize Deakin's intention in bringing them both to their feet. When he did the time for realization had long gone by.

His hands grasping Carlos's coat, Deakin flung himself violently backwards. Carlos, taken by surprise and completely off-balance on that icy surface, had no option but to topple after him. As they fell, Deakin doubled his legs until his knees almost touched his chin, got both feet into Carlos's midriff and kicked upward with all his strength. The forward velocity of Carlos's fall and the vicious upthrust from Deakin's legs combined with the strong downpull of his arms, broke Carlos's stranglehold and sent him, arms and legs flailing ineffectually and helplessly, catapulting over the side of the wagon, over the side of the bridge and into the depths of the ravine below.

Deakin reached quickly for the security of a ventilator and stared down into the gorge. Carlos, tumbling through the air in an almost grotesquely lazy slow motion, vanished into the snow-filled depths. As he disappeared, a long thin fading scream of terror reached up from the blackness below.

Deakin's were not the only ears to hear Carlos's last sound on earth. Henry, busy tending a pot of coffee on the stove, looked up sharply. He stood for a few moments in a tensely waiting position, then, when no other sound came, shrugged and returned to the coffee-pot.

Winded, breathing heavily and massaging his bruised neck – an action which gave his aching right shoulder as much pain as it gave his neck solace – Deakin clung for some time to the ventilator, then edged cautiously to the rear of the supply wagon and lowered himself on to the rear platform. He moved inside, lit another oil-lamp and continued his research. He opened two more of the Army Medical Corps boxes. As before, those contained Winchester ammunition. He came to a fifth, was about to pass it by when he noticed that it was slightly more elongated than the others. That was enough for Deakin to get his cold chisel working immediately. The box was jammed with stone-coloured gutta-percha bags, the type frequently employed for the transport of gunpowder.

Deakin decided to open one more box even though it seemed in every way identical to its predecessor. This one was packed with small cylindrical objects, each about eight inches in length, each wrapped in grey greased paper, presumably waterproof. Deakin pocketed two of these, extinguished the oil-lamp, moved forward and took his sheepskin jacket down from the circular observation window it had been blanketing off and was in the process of shrugging into it when, through the window, he saw the rear door of the second coach open and Henry appear. He was carrying a coffee-pot, two mugs and a lantern. He closed the door behind him and looked around in mild astonishment. Apparently it had not been in Carlos's nature to abandon his post.

Deakin didn't wait. He moved quickly down the aisle to the rear of the supply wagon, passed out on to the rear platform and took up position at one of the observation windows.

Henry, lantern held high, opened the door and advanced slowly into the supply wagon. He looked to his left and stood quite still, his face registering total disbelief, perfectly understandable in the circumstances; Henry had not looked to find six oiled wooden boxes with their lids cavalierly wrenched off to expose their contents of ammunition, gunpowder and blasting powder. Slowly, in a fashion not far removed from that of a somnambulist, Henry laid down the coffee-pot and mugs and moved slowly towards the rear of the supply wagon, where he stopped, eyes wide and mouth open, looking down at the three opened coffins, two with the Winchester rifles, the third with the mortal remains of the Reverend Peabody. Recovering from his temporary trance-like state, Henry looked around almost wildly, as if to reassure himself that he was not in the company of the deranged vandal responsible for what lay around him, hesitated, made to retrace his steps, changed his mind and made for the rear of the coach. Deakin, who was now becoming proficient in such matters, made for the roof of the coach.

Henry emerged on to the rear platform. Long seconds passed before his now clearly rather dazed mind could accept the evidence of his senses, or what remained of them. The expression of shocked and staring incredulity as he realized that the rest of the train was no longer there was so extreme as to be almost a parody of the real thing. He stood there like a man turned to stone. Suddenly volition returned. He whirled round and disappeared through the still open doorway. Deakin swung down and followed him, although at a rather more sedate pace.

Henry ran through the supply wagon, the passageway in the sleeping coach and finally the passageway in the first coach until he reached the officers' day compartment at the front where Deakin was supposedly safely bedded down for the night. Henry's instinct had been unerring. Deakin had flown. Henry wasted no time in expressing stupefaction or any other emotion – by that time he'd probably have been stupefied to find Deakin still there – but turned at once and ran back the way he had come. As he crossed from the first to the second coaches he had a great deal too many things on his mind even to consider looking upwards, but even had he done so it was highly unlikely that he would have seen Deakin crouched on the roof above. As Henry rushed into the passageway of the sleeping coach, leaving the door wide open behind him, Deakin swung down to the platform and waited with interest by the open doorway.

He hadn't long to wait. There came the sound of a frantic hammering on a door, then Henry's voice. Henry's voice sounded as Henry had looked, overwrought.

'God's sake, Major, come quickly. They're gone, they're all gone!'

'What the devil are you talking about?' O'Brien's voice was distinctly testy, the voice of one rudely awakened from sound slumber. 'Talk sense, man.'

'Gone, Major, gone. The two horse wagons – they're no longer there.'

'What? You're drunk.'

'Wish to God I was. Gone, I tell you. And the ammunition and explosives boxes have been forced open. And the coffins. And Carlos is gone. And so is Deakin.

No sign of either of them. I heard a scream, Major – '

Deakin didn't wait to hear more. He crossed to the second coach, passed through the dining compartment, stopped outside Marica's door, tested it, found it locked, used his keys, and went inside, closing the door securely behind him. A night-light, turned low, burned on a little table beside Marica's bunk. Deakin crossed to this, turned it up, placed a hand on the blanket-clad shoulder of the sleeping girl and shook gently. She stirred, turned, opened her eyes, opened them much wider still, then opened her mouth. A large hand closed over it –

'Don't. You'll die if you do.' Her eyes opened even wider and Deakin shook his head, trying to look encouraging, which was a pretty difficult thing to do in the circumstances. 'Not by my hand, ma'am.' He jerked his free thumb towards the door. 'Your friends out there. They're after me. When they get me, they'll kill me. Can you hide me?'

He removed his hand. Despite the racing pulse in her neck she was no longer terrified, but her eyes were still wary. Her lips moved without her speaking, then she said : 'Why should I?'

'You save my life. I'll save yours.'

She looked at him with little reaction, not so much dispassionately as without understanding, then slowly shook her head. Deakin twisted his belt until the underside showed, opened a buttoned compartment, extracted a card and showed it to her. She read it, at first uncomprehending; her eyes widened again, then she nodded and looked at him in slow understanding. There came the sound of voices from the passageway. Marica slipped from her bunk and gestured urgently to Deakin, who climbed in and pressed closely against the compartment partition, pulling the clothes over his head. Marica

137

quickly turned down the night-light and was just climing into the bunk when a knock came at the door. Mari
did not answer but instead busied herself with arrangi
the clothing on the bed to conceal Deakin as effective
as possible. The knock came again, more peremptori
this time.

Marica propped herself on an elbow and said in
sleepy voice: 'Who is it?'

'Major O'Brien, ma'am.'

'Come in, come in. The door's not locked.' The do
opened and O'Brien stood in the doorway, making
move to come further. Marica said in an indigna
voice: 'What on earth do you mean by disturbing me
this hour, Major?'

O'Brien was most apologetic. 'The prisoner Deaki
Miss Fairchild. He's escaped.'

'Escaped? Don't be ridiculous. Where could a m
escape to in this wilderness?'

'That's just the point, ma'am. There *is* no place
escape to. That's why we think he's still aboard the trai

Marica looked at him in cold disbelief. 'And y
thought that perhaps I – '

Hastily and at his most pacific O'Brien said: 'No, n
Miss Fairchild. It's just that he could have sneaked
here silently when you were asleep – '

'Well, he's not hiding under *my* bed.' There was co
siderable asperity in Marica's tone.

'I can see that, ma'am. Please excuse me.' O'Brien be
what was clearly an uncharacteristically rapid retre
and the sound of his footsteps was lost as he moved alo
the passageway. Deakin's head appeared from under t
clothes –

'Well now, ma'am.' Deakin's voice was frankly adm
ing. 'That was something. And you never even had

tell a lie. I'd never have believed – '

'Out! You're covered with snow from head to foot and I'm freezing.'

'No. You get out. Get out, get dressed and bring Colonel Claremont here.'

'Get dressed! With – with you lying – '

Deakin laid a weary forearm across his eyes 'My dear girl – that is to say, I mean, ma'am – I have other and less pleasant things to think of. You saw that card. Don't let anyone hear you talk to him. Don't let anyone see you bring him here. And don't tell him I'm here.'

Marica gave him a very old-fashioned speculative look but she didn't argue any more. There was something in Deakin's face that precluded further argument. She dressed quickly, left and returned within two minutes, followed by an understandably bewildered-looking Colonel Claremont.

As Marica closed the door behind them Deakin drew back the covers from his face and swung his legs over the edge of the bunk.

'Deakin! Deakin!' Claremont stared his disbelief. 'What in God's name – ' He broke off and reached for the Colt at his waist.

'Leave that damned gun alone.' Deakin said tiredly. 'You're going to have every chance to use it later. Not on me, though.'

He handed Claremont his card. Claremont took it hesitantly, read it, then read it a second time and third time. He said : ' "John Stanton Deakin . . . United States Government . . . Federal Secret Service . . . Allan Pinkerton." ' Claremont recovered his aplomb with remarkable speed and calmly handed the card back to Deakin. 'Mr Pinkerton I know personally. That's his signature. I know you too. Now. Or I know of you. In 1866 you were John Stanton. You were the man who broke open the $700,000 Adams Express robbery in that year.' Deakin nodded. 'What do you want me to do, Mr Deakin?'

'What does *he* want *you* – but you've only just met him, Colonel.' Marica was openly incredulous. 'How do you know that he – I mean, don't you *question* him or –'

'No one questions John Stanton Deakin, my dear.' Claremont's voice was almost gentle.

'But I've never even heard of –'

'We're not allowed to advertise,' Deakin said patiently. '*Secret* Service the card says. There's no time for questions. They're on to me now and neither of your lives is worth a burnt-out match.' He paused reflectively. 'That would still hold true even if they weren't on to me. But it's come earlier now. Every other person left alive on this train at this moment has only one ambition in life – to see *we* don't stay alive.' He opened the door a crack, listened, then closed it. 'They're up front, talking. Now's our one and only chance. Come on.' He ripped the sheets from Marica's bed and stuffed them under his jacket.

Claremont said: 'What do you want those for?'

'Later. Come on.'

'Come on?' Marica spoke almost wildly. 'My uncle! I can't leave –'

Deakin said very softly. 'I intend to see that the honourable and upright Governor, your beloved uncle, stands trial for murder, high treason and grand larceny.'

Marica looked at him in totally uncomprehending silence, her face registering almost a state of shock. Deakin eased open the door. A babble of excited raised voices could be heard from the officers' day compartment. Henry, at the moment, was holding the floor.

'Richmond! That's where I saw him. Richmond.

Henry sounded acutely unhappy. 'Sixty-three, it was. A Union espionage agent. I saw him just the once. He escaped. But that's him.'

'God! A Federal agent.' O'Brien's tone was vicious but the accompanying apprehension was more than just underlying. 'You know what this means, Governor?'

Apparently the Governor knew all too well what it meant. His voice was shaking and pitched abnormally high.

'Find him! For God's sake find him. Find him and kill him. Do you hear me? Kill him! Kill him!'

'I think he wants to kill me,' Deakin said in Marica's ear. 'Charming old boy, isn't he?'

Deakin hurried soft-footed down the passageway, a white-faced, badly shaken Marica behind with a singularly unflustered Claremont bringing up the rear. They walked quickly through the dining-room and moved out on to the rear platform. Wordlessly, Deakin gestured towards the roof. Claremont glanced at him in momentary puzzlement, then nodded his understanding. With an assist from Deakin he was swiftly on the roof, clinging to a ventilator with one hand while reaching for Marica with the other. Soon all three were on the roof, huddled together, their backs to the driving snow.

'This is dreadful!' Marica's voice was shaking, but it was with cold and not from fear. 'We'll freeze to death up here.'

'Don't speak ill of train roofs.' Deakin said reprovingly. 'They've become a kind of second home to me. Besides, at this moment, it's the safest place on this train. Bend down!'

At the urging of both his voice and arms they bent down as a thick broom of feathery conifer needles brushed their backs. Deakin said: 'The safest place if, that is, you watch out for those damned low-lying branches.'

'And now?' Claremont was very calm, with the fair
air of a man who expected to be enjoying himself an
moment.

'We wait. We wait and we listen.' Deakin stretche
himself out on the roof and put his ear to the ventilato
Claremont at once did the same. Deakin reached out a
arm and pulled Marica down beside them.

She said coldly: 'You don't have to keep your ar
round me.'

'It's the romantic surroundings,' Deakin explained
'I'm very susceptible to that sort of thing.'

'Are you indeed?' Her voice was icy as the night.

'I don't want you to fall off the damned train.' Sh
lapsed into hurt silence.

'They're there,' Claremont said softly. Deakin nodde

O'Brien, Pearce and Henry, all with guns in the
hands, stood in momentary indecision in the dining com
partment.

Pearce said: 'If Henry heard a scream and Deakin di
have a fight with Carlos, maybe they both fell off th
train and—'

In so far as it was possible for the Governor to run, h
came running into the compartment. Two yards and h
was out of breath.

'My niece! She's gone!'

There was a brief, baffled silence from which O'Brie
was the first to recover. He said to Henry: 'Go see
Colonel Claremont—no, I'll go myself.'

Deakin and Claremont exchanged glances, then Dea
kin twisted and peered over the rear edge just in time
see O'Brien crossing swiftly between the first and secor
coaches. O'Brien, Deakin noted, had forgotten the el
mentary courtesy of holstering his pistol before goir

calling on his commanding officer. Deakin moved back
to the ventilator, absent-mindedly putting his arm round
the girl's shoulders. If she had objections, she failed to
voice them.

Claremont said: 'You and Carlos had differences?'

'Some. On the roof of the supply wagon. He fell off.'

'Carlos? Fell off? That nice big cheerful man?'
Marica's capacity for absorbing fresh and increasingly
unwelcome information was about exhausted. 'But – but
he may be badly hurt. I mean, lying back there on the
track-side, perhaps freezing to death in this awful cold.'

'He's badly hurt all right. But he's not on the track-
side and he isn't feeling a thing. We were passing over a
bridge at the time. He fell a long, long way down to the
bottom of a ravine.'

'You killed him.' Deakin could barely catch the husky
words. 'But that's murder!'

'Every man needs a hobby.' Deakin tightened his grip
on her shoulders. 'Or perhaps you'd rather I was lying
at the bottom of that ravine? I damn nearly was.'

She was silent for a few moments, then said: 'I'm
sorry. I am a fool.'

'Yes,' Claremont said ungallantly. 'Well, Mr Deakin,
what's next?'

'We take over the locomotive.'

'We'd be safe there?'

'Once we've disposed of our friend Banlon we will.'
Claremont looked at him without understanding. 'I'm
afraid so, Colonel. Banlon.'

'I can't believe it.'

'The shades of the three men he's already killed would
believe it all right.'

'*Three* men?'

'To my certain knowledge.'

It took Claremont a very brief time only to come to terms with the fresh reality. He said in a calm voice: 'S he's armed?'

'I don't know. I think so. Anyway, Rafferty has h rifle with him. Banlon would use that – after shovin Rafferty over the side.'

'He could hear us coming? He could hold us off?'

'It's an uncertain world, Colonel.'

'We could take our stand in the train. In a passage way. In a doorway. I've got my revolver – '

'Hopeless. They're desperate men. With all respec Colonel, I doubt whether you could match either Pearc or O'Brien with a hand-gun. And even if you could hol them off there would still be an awful lot of gunfire. An the first shot Banlon hears he's on his guard. Nobod could get near his cab – and he'd drive straight throug to Fort Humboldt without stopping.'

'So? We'd be among friends.'

'I'm afraid not.' He held up a warning finger, looke cautiously over the rear edge of the roof in time to se O'Brien crossing from the second to the first coach. H put his ear to the ventilator again. From the tone of h voice O'Brien's relaxed urbanity appeared to have abar doned him.

'The Colonel's gone too! Henry, stay here, see no on passes you – either way. Shoot on sight. Kill on sigh Nathan, Governor – we'll start from the back and searc every inch of this damned train.'

Deakin gestured urgently forward but Claremont, o his knees now, was staring towards the rear of the trair

'The horse wagons! They're gone!'

'Later! Later! Come on.'

Soundlessly, the three edged their way along the centr line of the leading coach's roof. Arrived at the other en

Deakin lowered himself to the platform and peered through the coach's front observation window. Henry was clearly visible at the far end of the pasageway, strategically placed with his back to the side of the dining compartment, where his constantly moving eyes could cover both the front and rear approaches. Cradled in his right hand in an unpleasantly purposeful fashion was a Peacemaker Colt.

Deakin glanced upwards, put a finger, perhaps unnecessarily, to his lips, pointed to the interior of the coach, reached up and helped both Marica and Claremont on to the platform. Still silently, he reached out a hand to Claremont, who hesitated, then handed him his gun. Deakin made a downward patting motion with his hand to indicate that they should stay where they were, climbed over the safety rail, reached for the rear of the tender and transferred his weight to one of the buffers. Slowly he hoisted himself upwards until his eyes cleared the stacked cordwood at the rear of the tender.

Banlon was peering ahead through the driving window. Rafferty had the glowing fire-box open and was busily engaged in stoking it. Leaving the door open, he turned and made for the tender: Deakin's head swiftly disappeared from sight. Rafferty lifted two more baulks of cordwood and had hardly begun to move forward again when Deakin pulled himself upward until he was in full view of either of the two men who cared to turn round. He made his way quickly but with great care over the stacked cordwood, then lowered himself noiselessly to the floor of the tender.

Banlon had suddenly become very still. Something, almost certainly a fleeting reflection or movement in his driving window, had caught his attention. He looked slowly away from the window and glanced at Rafferty, who caught his eye at the same moment. Both men turned round and looked to the rear. Deakin was four feet away and the Colt in his hand was pointed at the middle of Banlon's body.

Deakin said to Rafferty: 'I see your rifle there. Don't try to get it. Read this.'

Reluctantly almost, Rafferty took the card from Deakin's hand, stopped and read it by the light from the firebox. He handed it back to Deakin, his face puzzled and uncertain.

Deakin said: 'Colonel Claremont and Miss Fairchild are on the first platform. Help them over here. Very, very quietly, Rafferty – if you don't want your head blown off.'

Rafferty hesitated, nodded and left. He was back within twenty seconds accompanied by Claremont and Marica. As they moved from the tender to the cab, Deakin moved towards Banlon, caught him by the lapels, thrust him back violently against the side of the cab and pushed the muzzle of the Colt, far from gently, into Banlon's throat.

'Your gun, Banlon. Vermin like you always have a gun.'

Banlon, who looked as if he were about to be sick at any moment, fought for breath against the pressure of the pistol. Under the circumstances, his attempt at outrage did considerable credit to his histrionic ability.

'What in God's name is the meaning of this? Colonel Claremont – '

Deakin jerked him forward, twisted him around, pushed Banlon's right hand up somewhere between the shoulder-blades and thrust him towards the steps and the open doorway on the right-hand side of the cab.

'Jump!'

Banlon's staring eyes reflected his horror. Through the driving snow he could just see a steep-sided rock-strewn gully rushing by. Deakin jabbed the Colt's muzzle hard against Banlon's back. 'Jump, I said.' Marica, shocked disbelief registering in her face, made to move towards Deakin; Claremont put out a restraining arm.

'The tool-box!' Banlon shouted. 'It's under the tool-box.'

Deakin stepped back, allowing Banlon to move into the safety of the cab. With his gun Deakin motioned him into a corner and said to Rafferty: 'Get it, will you?'

Rafferty glanced at Claremont, who nodded. The soldier felt beneath the tool-box and produced a revolver which he handed to Deakin, who took it and handed Claremont back his own gun. Claremont jerked his head in the direction of the rear of the tender and Deakin nodded.

'They're no fools. It won't take them long to figure that if we're not in the train we must be on top of it and if we're not there there's only one other place we can be. Anyway, the marks we left on the roof will give us away.' Deakin turned to Rafferty. 'Point your gun at Banlon and keep pointing it. If he moves, kill him.'

'*Kill* him?'

'You wouldn't try to just *wound* a rattlesnake, would you? Banlon's more deadly than any rattlesnake. Kill him, I say. He's going to die anyway. By the rope.'

'Me? The rope!' Banlon's face twisted. 'I don't know who you think you are, Deakin, but the law says –'

There was no warning. Deakin took one long stride forward and struck him viciously, back-handed, to send him stumbling against the controls, blood welling immediately from his nose and mouth.

'I am the law.'

EIGHT

Banlon dabbed ineffectually at nose and mouth with
wad of very unhygienic waste. His self-ministrations ha
no noticeable effect, the blood continued to flow copi
ously. Banlon's normally wizened face now looked eve
more scraped and drawn, the brown parchment of th
skin was several degrees paler and his eyes darted con
tinuously from side to side, a trapped wild animal lookin
for a means of escape that did not exist. Mainly his eye
flitted from Deakin to Claremont and back again but h
found no comfort there: the faces of both men wer
devoid of pity.

'The end of the road,' Claremont said. 'Live by th
sword and you'll die by the same. John Stanton Deaki
is the law, Banlon, a secret agent of the Federal Goverr
ment. You will know what that means.'

Clearly Banlon knew all too well. His weasel fac
looked, if possible, even more hunted than before
Deakin said to Rafferty: 'Through the body, not th
head. We don't want all those nasty ricochets flying abou
inside the cab.'

He turned his back on the company, moved into th
tender and started throwing aside the cordwood from th
right-hand rear corner. The eyes of Marica and Banlo
did not once leave him. Claremont, Colt cocked, divide
his attention between Deakin and Banlon: Rafferty
sticking to his brief, had eyes only for Banlon.

Deakin, his task evidently finished, straightened an
stood to one side. Marica performed the classic gestur

of putting her hand to her mouth, the dark smoky eyes huge in an ashen face. Claremont stared at the two crumpled uniform-clad forms, the upper parts of whose bodies had been exposed.

'Oakland! Newell!'

Deakin said bleakly to Banlon: 'Like I said, the rope.' He turned to Claremont. 'You know now why you couldn't find Oakland and Newell in Reese City. They never left the train.'

'They found out something they shouldn't have found out?'

'Whatever it was they found, it was in this cab. They must have been killed in this cab – you can't carry two dead officers along a platform busy with soldiers. I don't think they could have seen anything suspicious or incriminating. Not in a cab. Probably heard someone, Banlon and someone else, discussing some very odd things and mounted the cab to investigate, the last mistake they ever made.'

'Henry. That was the someone else. Banlon himself told me that they'd sent the stoker – Jackson – into town while they –'

'While they covered up the bodies of the dead men with cordwood. That's why poor Jackson had to die. He discovered the bodies.' Deakin stooped and carefully replaced some of the cordwood to cover the men. 'I think Banlon was scared that they were using wood too fast and that Jackson would find them, so he plied Jackson with tequila in the hope of making him paralytic and then disposing of the bodies while Jackson snored his head off. But all that happened was that the drink made Jackson careless in the unloading. He pulled all the wood from one corner and discovered the bodies. Then Banlon had to kill him. A heavy spanner, probably; but that

149

didn't kill him.'

'Before God, Colonel. I don't know what this madman's talking about.' Banlon's voice was a high-pitched whine, he was projecting the image of a cornered animal more successfully than ever. Claremont ignored him, his entire attention was on Deakin. 'Go on.'

'When Jackson hit the side of the gorge, death was instantaneous. But there was a deep cut on the back of the neck that had bled badly.'

'And dead men don't bleed.'

'Dead men don't bleed. Banlon tied a cleaning rag to Jackson's wrist, threw him out over the bridge, stopped the train, made marks in front of the cab window to show Jackson had been there and then told the tale.'

Banlon's voice was hoarse, naked fear in it. 'You can't prove any of this!'

'That's so. I can't prove either that you faked control-lever trouble to give enough time for the telegraph lines back to Reese City to be cut.'

Claremont said slowly: 'I saw Banlon adjusting the steam throttle in Reese City –'

'Slackening it, more like. Nor can I prove that he made a premature stop for fuel to allow an explosive charge to be fitted behind the front coupling of the leading troop coach – timed to go off near the top of the steepest climb in the mountains. It's easy now to guess why nobody jumped off or tried to stop the runaway. When we recover the wreckage you can be sure that we'll find that all the doors were locked from outside and that the brakeman had been murdered.'

'On purpose?' Marica whispered. 'Those men were all – murdered?'

Four shots rang out in swift succession followed, at once by the screaming ricochet of bullets as they struck the ironwork of the cab and went screaming off into the darkness and the snow; none, almost unbelievably, ricocheted about the interior of the cab.

'Down!' Deakin shouted. In unison they threw themselves to the floor of the cab and tender – all except Banlon. Banlon's life was already forfeit. A heavy eighteen-inch wrench miraculously appeared in his hand, sliced down in a murderous arc and struck the prone Rafferty a crushing blow on the side of the head. Banlon wrenched the rifle from the already powerless hands and swung round. He said to Claremont, who had his revolver pointing towards the rear of the tender : 'Don't move,' and to Deakin, whose gun was still in his belt : 'I wish you would.'

Neither man moved.

'Lay down your guns.'

They laid down their guns.

'On your feet. Hands high.'

The three rose, Deakin and Claremont with raised arms. Banlon said to Marica : 'You heard.

She didn't appear to have done so. She was staring unbelievingly down at Rafferty. Quite clearly, he was dead. Banlon shifted the rifle slightly. 'Last chance, lady.'

Like a person in a dream world she slowly lifted her hands. Banlon transferred his attention to Deakin and as he did so Marica's right hand moved slowly until it was behind one of the suspended oil-lamps. If Deakin had seen the stealthy movement no slightest hint of it showed in his face or eyes. Her hand gradually closed on the lamp.

Banlon said : 'I don't know why you brought those white sheets but they're going to be mighty useful. Climb up on the cordwood there and wave one. Now!'

Marica's hand lifted the lamp clear and her arm jerked

convulsively forward. Out of the corner of his eye Banlon saw the blur of light come towards him. He whirled, moving sideways, but was too late to prevent the lamp from striking him in the face. He retained hold of the rifle but was off-balance for all of two seconds, more time than a man like Deakin would ever need. His headlong dive caught Banlon in the midriff, sending the rifle clattering to the floor and Banlon staggering back to crash with stunning force against the boiler. Deakin followed like a big cat, caught Banlon by the throat and smashed his head twice against the metalwork.

Deakin's face was no longer without expression. As his eyes shifted to the left and down and rested momentarily on Rafferty's body his face was savage and bitter and almost inhuman and for the first time Marica looked on him with fear. Deakin returned his attention to Banlon. Banlon could already have been dead but Deakin neither knew nor cared. Once again Banlon's head thudded against the boiler, almost certainly crushing the occiput. Deakin lifted the man high, took two steps and threw him out over the side of the cab.

Pearce and O'Brien, guns in hands, were on the leading coach's front platform. Suddenly, both their gazes jerked sideways and they had just time to identify Banlon's tumbling body before it disappeared into the darkness. They stared at each other, then moved hastily off the platform inside the coach.

In the cab, Deakin's temporary expression of implacability had been replaced by the habitual mask of impassivity. He said to Marica : 'Go on. I know. I shouldn't have done it.'

'Why not?' she said reasonably. 'You said you couldn't prove a thing.'

For the second time that night Deakin's expression

slipped. He stared at her in total astonishment. He said carefully: 'We may have more in common than you think.'

She smiled at him sweetly. 'How do you know what I think?'

In the officers' day compartment O'Brien, Pearce, Henry and the Governor were holding what appeared to be a council of war. At least, the first three were. The Governor, a brimming whisky glass in his hand, was staring at the wood stove; the expression of misery on his face was profound.

'This is terrible!' His voice was a low moan. 'Terrible. I'm ruined. Oh my God.'

O'Brien said savagely: 'You didn't think it terrible when I found out what kind of man you were, that you'd rigged elections and spent a fortune in bribes to become Governor and suggested you come in with Nathan and myself. You didn't think it terrible when you suggested Nathan here would be the ideal agent and appointed him personally to deal with the Indian reservations. You didn't think it terrible when you insisted on your share of half of all we made. You make me feel violently ill, Governor Fairchild.'

'I didn't think we'd get involved in anything like this,' the Governor muttered drearily. 'All this killing. All this murder. What peace of mind is there in this for an honest man?' He ignored or did not hear O'Brien's incredulous exclamation. 'You didn't tell me you wanted my niece as a hostage in case there was trouble with her father. You didn't tell me –'

Pearce said with feeling: 'God knows what I'd like to tell you. But I have more to think of.'

'You're supposed to be men of action.' Fairchild tried

to be scathing but only succeeded in sounding depressed
'Why don't you *do* something?'

O'Brien looked at him in contempt.

'Do what, you old fool? Have you seen that barricade
of cordwood they've erected at the back of the tender?
It would take a cannon shell to go through it, while
they're probably peering through a chink, gun in hand
ready to pick off the first of us to go through that door
At six feet,' he added with gloomy finality, 'they can
hardly miss.'

'You don't have to make a frontal attack. Go to the
back of this coach, climb up and make your approach
over the roof. That way you'll be able to look *down* on
anyone in the tender.'

O'Brien pondered, then said: 'Maybe you're not such
an old fool after all.'

While Deakin acquainted himself with the controls
Claremont stoked the fire and Marica, sitting on some
cordwood with a tarpaulin over her shoulders to protect
her from the snow, kept a close watch on the front of the
leading coach through a strategically placed chink in the
cordwood barricade. Claremont closed the fire-box and
straightened.

'So Pearce it was?'

'Yes,' Deakin said. 'Pearce it was. He's been on our
suspect list for a long time. It's true he was once an
Indian fighter but he moved over to the other side six
years ago. But to the world at large he's still Uncle Sam's
man keeping a fatherly eye on the reservations. Whisky
and guns. Fatherly!'

'O'Brien?'

'Nothing against him. Every detail of his military
record known. A fine soldier but a rotten apple – remem

er that big reunion scene in Reese City with Pearce,
recalling the good old days at Chattanooga in '63?
O'Brien was there all right. Pearce was never within a
thousand miles of it – he was an Indian scout for one of
the six cavalry companies raised by what became the
new State of Nevada the following year. So that made
O'Brien a bad one, too.'

'Which must go for the Governor as well?'

'What else? He's weak and avaricious and a mani-
ulator of some note.'

'But he'll hang from the same tree?'

'He'll hang from the same tree.'

'You suspected everyone.'

'My nature. My job.'

'Why not me?'

'You didn't want Pearce aboard. That put you in the
clear. But *I* wanted him aboard – and me. It wasn't hard
– not with those splendid "Wanted" notices the Service
provided.'

'You fooled me.' Claremont sounded bitter but not
rancorous. 'Everyone fooled me. The Government or the
Army *might* have taken me into their confidence.'

'Nobody fooled you. We suspected there *might* be
something wrong at Humboldt so it was thought better
to have two strings to the bow. When I joined this train
I knew no more about what was going on at Humboldt
than you did.'

'But now you know?'

'Now I know.'

'Deakin!' Deakin whirled round as the shout came
from behind him, his hand reaching for the gun in his
belt. 'There's a gun lined up on the little lady. Don't try
anything, Deakin.'

Deakin didn't try anything. Pearce was sitting on the

roof of the leading coach, his feet dangling over the fron
edge, a very steady Colt in his hand and his saturnin
hawk-like face creased in a very unfriendly smile.

Deakin kept his hands well away from his body whic
seemed a doubly advisable thing to do for, a few fee
behind Pearce on the roof, he could now make ou
O'Brien also, inevitably with pistol in hand. Deakin
called : 'What do you want me to do?'

'That's more like it, Mr Secret Service man.' Pearc
sounded almost jovial. 'Stop the train.'

Deakin turned towards the controls and said *sott*
voce : 'Stop the train, the man said.'

He eased the brake very gently as he closed the throttle
Suddenly, in a convulsive movement, he closed the brake
all the way. The locomotive wheels locked solid and ther
came a series of violently metallic crashes as the buffer
of the tender and the following coaches came into jarrin
successive contact.

The effect for the two gunmen on the roof was disas
trous. The combination of the sudden deceleration an
the violent jolting sent the seated Pearce sliding helplessl
forward on the ice-coated roof to pitch wildly downward
on to the platform beneath, his gun spinning away on t
the track-side as he clutched at the safety rail to sav
himself. Further back on the roof O'Brien was sprawle
out broadside on the length of the coach as he clun
tightly to a ventilator to prevent himself from going th
same way as Pearce.

Deakin shouted : 'Down!' He released the brake
opened the throttle wide and dived towards the tende
Claremont was already sprawled on the cab floor whil
Marica was sitting on the floor of the tender with
pained expression on her face. Deakin risked a quic

glance over the cordwood barricade at the rear of the tender.

Pearce, already on his feet, was moving very quickly indeed into the shelter of the leading coach. O'Brien, face bitter and masked in rage, was lining up his pistol. Flame stabbed from the muzzle. For Deakin, the shot, the metallic clang as the bullet struck metal and the whine of the ricochet came as one. Almost as a reflex action he grabbed the nearest baulk of cordwood and, without exposing himself to O'Brien's fire, hurled it upwards and backwards.

O'Brien had no target to fire at, but then he did not think he required one. A haphazardly ricocheting spent shell inside that confined metallic space could be just as deadly as a direct hit. As he eased the pressure on the trigger, the expression on his face changed from anger to alarm; the cordwood baulk rapidly approaching him seemed as large as a tree trunk. Still retaining his grip on the ventilator, he flung himself to one side but too late to prevent the baulk of timber striking him on the shoulder with numbing force: his gun flew wide. Unaware that O'Brien was disarmed, Deakin continued to throw baulks of wood as fast as he could stoop and straighten. O'Brien managed to avoid some of the missiles and fend off others, but was unable to prevent himself from being struck by quite a number. He made an awkward, scuttling, crablike retreat towards the rear of the roof of the first coach and thankfully lowered himself to the shelter of the rear platform.

In the tender Deakin stood up, risked a quick first glance, then a longer one to the rear. The coast was clear. Both the front platform and the roof of the leading coach were deserted. He turned to Marica.

'Hurt?'

She rubbed herself tenderly. 'Only where I sat down suddenly.'

Deakin smiled and looked at Claremont. 'You?'

'Only my dignity.'

Deakin nodded, eased the throttle, picked up Rafferty's rifle, moved towards the rear of the tender and began to arrange a fresh gap in the cordwood barricade.

In the day compartment the Governor and his three companions were holding their second council of war. There was for the moment a certain aura of frustration, if not precisely defeatism. Governor Fairchild had the same brimming glass – or another brimming glass – of whisky in his hand. His expression as he gazed into the glowing wood stove was nervously unhappy in the extreme. O'Brien and Pearce, the latter just replacing a decanter on the centre of the table between them, wore the expressions of two very tough, very competent men who were not accustomed to being routed so completely and so easily. Henry, also with a glass in his hand, stood at a respectful distance; his expression was, if that were possible, more lugubrious than ever.

Pearce said savagely: 'Any more clever ideas, Governor?'

'The conception was mine. The execution was yours. Is it my fault he out-smarted you? By God, if I were twenty years younger –'

'You're not,' said O'Brien. 'So shut up.'

Henry said diffidently: 'We've a crate of blasting powder. We could throw a stick –'

'If you've nothing better to suggest, you'd better shut up, too. We need this train to take us back east.'

They relapsed into a brooding silence, a silence which

came to an abrupt end as the whisky decanter shattered and sent the alcohol and razor-edged slivers of glass flying across the compartment. The sharp crack of a rifle was clearly heard. The Governor took his hand away from his cheek and stared uncomprehendingly at the blood. There came a second crack and Pearce's black hat flew across the compartment. Suddenly, there was no more incomprehension. All four men flung themselves to the floor and crawled hurriedly towards the passageway leading to the dining compartment. Three more bullets thudded into the day compartment, but by the time the last of those had arrived the compartment had been vacated.

Deakin withdrew his rifle from the cordwood barricade, stood up, took Marica by the arm and led her into the locomotive cab. He eased the throttle some more, picked up the dead Rafferty, carried him to the tender and covered him with a piece of tarpaulin before returning to the cab.

Claremont said : 'I'd better get back on watch, then.'

'No need. They won't bother us again tonight.' He peered closely at Claremont. 'Only your dignity hurt, eh?' He lifted Claremont's left arm and looked at the hand which was bleeding profusely. 'Clean it with snow, ma'am, please, then bandage it with a strip of that sheet.' He returned his attention to the track ahead. The train was doing no more than fifteen miles an hour, a safe maximum in the very restricted visibility conditions. Unenthusiastically, he set about stoking the fire-box.

Claremont winced as Marica cleaned the wound. He said : 'Back there on the roof you said there would be no friends at the Fort.'

'There will be some – under lock and key. The Fort's been taken over. Sepp Calhoun, for a certainty. With the help, probably, of the Paiutes.'

'Indians! What's in it for Indians – except reprisals'

'There's a lot in it for the Indians – and no reprisal either. Not once they've received the payment we'r carrying aboard this train.'

'Payment?'

'In the supply wagon. Why Doctor Molyneux died Why Peabody died. Molyneux said he was going t examine the medical supplies – so Molyneux had to die

'Had to?'

'There's no medicine on this train. The medical crate are stuffed with rifle ammunition.'

Claremont watched Marica complete the bandagin of his hand. After a long pause he said: 'I see. And th Reverend?'

'The Reverend? I doubt whether Peabody has eve seen the inside of a church. He's been a Union an Federal agent for the last twenty years, my partner fo the last eight of those.'

Claremont said carefully: 'He's been what?'

'They caught him opening up a coffin. You know, fo the cholera victims.'

'I know. I know what the coffins are for.' Claremor sounded testy but the impatience in his voice probabl stemmed from his confusion.

'There's as much cholera in Fort Humboldt as ther are brains in my head.' Deakin, with little or no just fication, sounded thoroughly disgusted with himsel 'Those coffins are full of Winchester rifles, repeaters, leve action tubular magazines.'

'No such thing.'

'There is now.'

'How come I've never heard of them?'

'Few people have – outside the factory. Productio

began only four months ago, none has been on sale yet –
but the first four hundred were stolen from the factory.
Now we know where all those stolen arms are, don't we?'

'I don't know where *I* am. Coming or going. I'm lost.
What happened to the horse-wagons, Mr Deakin?'

'I detached them.'

'Inevitably. Why?'

Deakin glanced at the gauge. 'A moment. We're losing
pressure.'

There was no easing of pressure in the comparative
safety of the dining compartment where Fairchild and
the others were holding their third council of war. It was
a council singularly lacking in animation, or, for that
matter, conversation. For the most part the Governor,
O'Brien and Pearce sat in silent gloom, which another
bottle of whisky they had obtained from somewhere
seemed powerless to dispel, while Henry dispiritedly
stoked the wooden stove.

The Governor stirred. 'Nothing? Can you think of
nothing?'

O'Brien was curt. 'No.'

'There *must* be an answer.'

Henry straightened from the stove. 'Begging the
Governor's pardon, we don't need an answer.'

'Oh, do be quiet,' O'Brien said wearily.

Henry had his say to say and refused to be quiet. 'We
don't need an answer because there isn't any question.
The only question *could* be, what happens if we don't
stop him. Well, it's simple. He just drives on till he's safe
and sound with his friends in Fort Humboldt.'

There was a quickening of interest, a long and thoughtful silence, then O'Brien said slowly: 'By God, I do
believe you're right, Henry. Just because he knows we're

running guns to the Indians we've assumed that he knows all about us, what we *really* have in mind. Of *course* he doesn't. How could he? Nobody does. Impossible — nobody but us have been in touch with the Fort.

'What else?' O'Brien said expansively. 'Well, gentlemen, it's a bitter night. I suggest we just let Deakin get right on with his driving. He seems quite competent.'

Beaming broadly, the Governor reached for the bottle. He said with happy anticipation : 'White Hand will certainly give him a warm welcome when we arrive at the Fort.'

White Hand was, at that moment, quite a long distance from the Fort and increasing the distance between them by the minute. The snow was still falling but not so heavily; the wind was still blowing but not so strongly. Behind White Hand, two or three score heavily muffled horsemen cantered rapidly along the base of a broad and winding valley. White Hand turned his head and looked slightly to his left and upwards. Already, above the mountains, there were the beginnings of a lightening of the sky to the east.

White Hand swung in the saddle, gestured to the east and beckoned his men on, urgently, impatiently. The Paiutes began to string out as they increased speed along the valley floor.

Deakin, too, could see the first signs of the pre-dawn as he straightened from the open fire-box. He glanced at the steam-gauge, nodded in satisfaction and closed the door of the fire-box. Claremont and Marica, both pale-faced and showing unmistakable signs of exhaustion, occupied the two bucket seats in the cab. Deakin himself could easily have felt the same way but he could not yet allow himself the luxury of being tired. As much to keep himself alert and occupied as for any other reason, Deakin resumed where he had left off.

'Yes. The horse wagons. I had to cut those loose. Indians – almost certainly the Paiutes under White Hand – are going to try to intercept and ambush this train at the entrance to Breakheart Pass. I know Breakheart Pass. They'll be forced to leave their horses at least a mile away – and I don't want them to have any more horses ready to hand.'

'Ambush? Ambush?' Claremont was a man groping in the dark. 'But I thought the Indians were working hand in hand with those – those renegades back there.'

'And so indeed they are. But they're under the impression that the attempt to detach the troop wagons failed – and, for them, those troops must be destroyed. *had* to get the Indians out of the Fort – otherwise we could never get in.'

Claremont said carefully: 'They're under the impression that –'

'The missing telegraph. It was missing because I hid it. In the haybox in the first horse wagon. When we were stopped last night and I was fuelling this damned fire-box I took time off to use it. They thought I was O'Brien.'

Claremont looked at him for a long moment. 'You've been very busy, Mr Deakin.'

'I haven't been all that idle.'

'But why, why, why?' Marica spread her hands helplessly. 'Why for the sake of a few crates of rifles should Fort Humboldt be taken over? Why should the Paiutes be attacking the train? Why the killings, the massacre of those soldiers? Why should my uncle, O'Brien and Pearce be risking their lives, wrecking their careers –'

'Those coffins aren't arriving empty at Fort Humboldt

and by the same token and for the same reason they won't be leaving empty either.

Claremont said : 'But you said there was no cholera –'

'No cholera. But there's something else at Fort Humboldt, something quite different from cholera, something for which men will sell their lives, their honour, their souls. Have you ever heard of four men called Mackay Fair, O'Brien – no relation of our friend back there – and Flood ?'

Claremont looked down at the blood seeping slowly through the makeshift bandage. 'The names sound familiar.'

'Those are the four men who struck the Big Bonanza earlier this year on the Comstock. To our certain knowledge there's already been ten million dollars' worth taken out of the ground. There's only one way this metal can be shipped east – on this railroad. And, of course there's also the regular gold bullion transport from the Californian fields. Both sets of bullion *have* to funnel through Fort Humboldt. It's my guess that, at this moment, there's more gold and silver bullion in Fort Humboldt than in any place outside the Federal vaults.'

Claremont said : 'It's just as well that I'm already sitting down.'

'Make yourself at home. As you know, the state governor is notified whenever there's going to be a large-scale bullion transport through his territory and it's up to him to notify either the military or civilian authorities to provide the guard. In this case Fairchild notified neither Instead he notified O'Brien, who notified Pearce, who notified Calhoun, who hired the services of the Paiute for a stated reward. It's all very simple, isn't it ?'

'And the bullion was going back in those coffins ?'

'How else ? Can *you* imagine a safer, a more foolproof

form of transport? Nobody's going to open up coffins – especially the coffins of men who have died of cholera. If need be, those bullion coffins could even be buried with full military honours – to be dug up the following night, of course.'

Claremont shook his head. His spirit seemed to have left him, he was a man close to despair. 'All those murdering Paiutes, heaven knows how many of them, those desperadoes in the coaches behind us, Calhoun and his renegades waiting for us in Fort Humboldt –'

'Don't worry,' Deakin said comfortingly. 'We'll think of something.'

Marica looked at him with a coldly appraising eye. 'I'm sure you'll think of something, Mr Deakin.'

'As a matter of fact, I already have.'

NINE

The aptly named Breakheart Pass, a barren and waterless gully, carried the railway line up to a small divide. The left or southern hand of the gully was bordered by an almost vertical cliff; the right-hand side by a fairly shallow slope leading down to the long dead watercourse, a course liberally strewn with large boulders which offered splendid cover – splendid, that was, for men but quite useless for horses. The nearest shelter of any other kind was offered by a thick clump of pines a mile distant across the valley. It was within the confines of this copse that White Hand waved his weary troop of horsemen to a grateful halt.

White Hand dismounted. He pointed to the boulder-strewn gully. 'There the train will stop. There we will hide. We must go there on foot.' He turned to two of his men. 'The horses. Keep them here. Take them even deeper into the woods. They must not be seen.'

In the dining compartment of the train Henry sat by the wood stove, drowsing. Fairchild, O'Brien and Pearce, seated and with their heads resting on their forearms, were asleep or appeared to be asleep over the dining tables. On the footplate, Deakin, very far from being asleep, was peering ahead through the cab window; snow was still falling and the visibility was poor. Marica, equally wide awake, was making the final adjustments to the white sheet which was so wrapped round Colonel Claremont that, his unencumbered arms apart, he appeared to be cocooned from head to foot. Deakin beckoned to him and pointed ahead.

'Breakheart Pass coming up. Maybe two miles to go. For you, one mile. See that big clump of pines to the right of the track?' Claremont nodded. 'They'll have hidden their horses there. There'll be guards.' He nodded to Rafferty's rifle which Claremont held in his hands. *Don't* give them a sporting chance. *Don't* give them an even break.'

Claremont shook his head slowly and said nothing. His face was no less implacable than that of Deakin.

White Hand and another Indian were crouched behind a craggy rock on the boulder-strewn right-hand slope of the gully. They were staring down towards the lower, easternmost entrance to the pass. The thinly falling snow let them see as far as the furthest bend of the track; so far there was nothing to be seen. Suddenly the other Indian reached out and touched White Hand on the shoulder. Both men turned their heads slightly and adopted an intensely listening attitude. Far off, faintly but unmistakably, the puffing of a straining locomotive engine could be heard. White Hand glanced at his companion and nodded, just once.

Deakin reached under his coat and brought out the two sticks of blasting powder he had earlier filched from the supply wagon. One of these he carefully placed inside the tool-box, the other he held in his hand. With his free hand he gently eased the steam throttle all the way off. At once, the train began to slow down.

O'Brien woke with a start, moved swiftly to the nearest window, hastily cleared away the condensation and peered out. Almost at once he turned to Pearce.

'Wake up! Wake up! We're stopping! Nathan, know[s]
where we are?'

'Breakheart Pass.' The two men looked questioning[l]
at one another. Fairchild stirred, sat upright and cam[e]
to the window. He said uneasily: 'What's that devil u[p]
to now?'

Deakin was indeed up to something. With the train no[w]
almost brought to a complete standstill, he ignited th[e]
tube of blasting powder in his hand, judged his momen[t]
to what he regarded as a nicety, then tossed it out of th[e]
right-hand cab opening. At the same moment Claremon[t]
moved on to the steps of the left-hand side of the ca[b]
Pearce, O'Brien, Fairchild and Henry, all with their face[s]
pressed to the window, recoiled involuntarily and thre[w]
up defensive hands as there came a blinding flash of ligh[t]
and the flat sharp crack of an explosion immediately out[-]
side. The window did not shatter and after a moment o[r]
two they pressed close to it again. But by this time Clare[-]
mont had dropped off the left-hand side of the ca[b]
rolled down the embankment and come to rest at it[s]
foot. Wrapped in the white sheeting, he was almos[t]
entirely invisible and remained quite motionless. Deaki[n]
jerked the throttle open again.

The bafflement of the four men in the dining compart[-]
ment was of a lesser nature altogether than that of Whit[e]
Hand and his Indian companion. White Hand said un[-]
certainly: 'It may be that our friends wanted to warn u[s]
of their approach. See, they are moving again.'

'Yes. And I see something else.' The other India[n]
jumped to his feet. 'The troop wagons! The soldie[r]
wagons! They're not there!'

'Get down, fool!' White Hand's habitual impassivit[y]
had, for the moment, completely deserted him. His fac[e]

was baffled, uncomprehending, as he saw that the train, now well into Breakheart Pass, clearly consisted of no more than three coaches.

O'Brien's face was now equally uncomprehending. He said: 'How the hell should *I* know what he's up to? The man's a lunatic.'

Fairchild said: 'You could try to find out, couldn't you?'

Pearce handed Fairchild one of his guns. 'Tell you what, Governor. You find out.'

The Governor grabbed the gun. For that brief passing moment he was clearly out of his mind. 'Very well, then. I shall.'

He took the gun, moved forward, opened the front door of the leading coach no more than a crack and slid an apprehensive eye round the edge. A second later there was the boom of a Colt and a bullet struck the coach less than a foot from his head: Fairchild withdrew with speed, banging the door behind him, his momentary period of insanity clearly behind him. Severely shaken, he re-entered the dining compartment.

Pearce said: 'Well, what did you find out?'

The Governor said nothing. He threw the gun on the table and made for the whisky bottle.

Up front, Deakin said: 'Company?'

'My uncle.' Marica examined the still smoking Colt with aversion.

'Get him?'

'No.'

'Pity.'

Claremont, still swathed in his white camouflage, inched slowly towards the edge of the embankment and hitched a wary eye over the top. The train, almost a mile away by that time, was well into the pass. He scanned the boulders in the dry watercourse ahead but could detect no sign of movement. He had not expected to see any, not yet; White Hand was far too experienced to make his presence known until the last moment possible. Claremont then looked across the valley to the distant clump of pine trees. If Deakin were right and horses there were, that was where the horses would be held in concealment; and Claremont no longer questioned Deakin's judgment. The approach to the pines would be difficult but not impossible : a smaller branching watercourse led up to the very edge of the copse and if he could reach the foot of this dry gully unobserved he should be under concealment for the rest of the way. The only danger lay in crossing the railway line, and while he was far too experienced a soldier to discount the possibility of any danger, he thought that the odds on a safe traverse of the track lay in his favour. The guard or guards in charge of the horses would, in the normal course of events, be taking a lively interest in what was happening, or what was about to happen across the valley. But their attention would almost certainly be fixed on the train and the hidden Paiutes and those were now a mile away to his left. Besides, it was still only dawn and the snow had not yet ceased to fall. Claremont did not hesitate, if for no other reason than that he knew that there were no options left open to him. Wraith-like, and using only his elbows and knees, he began to slither across the track.

Deakin eased back the throttle. Marica, from her observation post at the back of the tender, spared him a brief glance. 'Stopping?'

'Slowing.' He indicated the right-hand side of the cab.

'Leave the tender and get down there. On the floor.'

Hesitantly, she moved forward. 'You think there'll be shooting?'

'Well, there won't be too many rose petals thrown, and that's a fact.'

The train was now crawling along at between ten and fifteen miles an hour but clearly was not about to come to a complete halt, a fact that was becoming increasingly obvious to White Hand. His face registered at first faint puzzlement, then exasperation, then finally outright anger.

'The fools!' he said. 'The fools! Why don't they stop?' He jumped to his feet, waving his arm. The train continued on its way. White Hand shouted to his warriors to follow him. They all broke concealment and came running and stumbling up the slope as quickly as the shingly and snow-covered terrain would permit them. Deakin judiciously opened the throttle a notch or two.

Once again O'Brien, Pearce, the Governor and Henry were peering with what was by now a degree of justifiable anxiety through the window. Pearce said: 'White Hand! White Hand and his braves! What in God's name is the meaning of this?' He ran towards the rear platform, the others closely behind him. As they arrived there the train perceptibly began to slow.

Fairchild said: 'We could jump for it now. White Hand could give us cover and –'

'Fool!' Whatever respect Pearce might ever have had for the governor of his state had clearly diminished to vanishing point. 'That's just exactly what he's inviting us to do. It's still a long, long walk to Fort Humboldt.' He waved to the rear and pointed towards the driving cab. White Hand waved a return acknowledgment, turned and shouted some unheard order. Immediately a score of rifles were levelled.

Deakin dropped to the floor of the cab as a fusillade of bullets struck the locomotive, then, in a momentary lull in the firing, risked a quick glance through the footplate doorway. The Indians, running as they reloaded, were clearly gaining. Once again, Deakin opened the throttle slightly.

O'Brien said with increasing unease: 'What in hell's name is Deakin playing at? He could leave them behind if he—'

He and Pearce stared at each other.

Claremont, safely arrived in the shelter of the wood, was moving swiftly and stealthily through the trees, circling so as to approach from the rear. The guards, he was certain, would be at the lower edge of the wood, watching the scene across the valley, which meant that their backs would be towards him. From the implacable expression on his face it was clear that Claremont had no compunction in the world about gunning down unsuspecting men from the rear; far too many lives, not to mention a fortune in bullion and all his men he had so recently lost, made any consideration of fair play seem totally irrelevant.

There were about sixty horses all told, none of them hobbled or tied — Indian ponies were as well trained as those of the United States Cavalry. Claremont picked out what he thought would be the three most likely horses — the rest he would stampede — and slowly worked his way through them. They neither whinnied nor neighed, some glanced incuriously at him, some not at all — despite the thickness of their coats, they were all clearly preoccupied with their own frozen miseries.

The guards — there were two of them — stood at the

very edge of the wood, just beyond the last of the horses, looking speculatively at each other as they listened to the now desultory gunfire from across the valley. Because of the cushioning effect of the snow, the occasional restless stamping of the horses, and the Indians' complete absorption with the running battle now almost two miles away, Claremont was able to approach within twenty feet before taking up position behind the sturdy bole of a pine. At that short distance the use of the rifle seemed superfluous. He laid his rifle silently against the trunk of the tree and brought out his Colt.

Aboard the train, both Pearce and O'Brien gestured frantically to the rear, pointing repeatedly towards the distant pine wood and motioning that White Hand and his men should return there. The Indian chief, comprehending, stopped in his tracks and indicated that his men should do the same. He wheeled and pointed to the pine wood.

'The horses!' White Hand shouted. 'Back to the horses!' He took just one running step, then stopped abruptly. The two distant revolver shots carried very clearly in the freezing air. White Hand, his face impassive, tapped two of his men on the shoulders. They set off at a jog-trot towards the pine wood, not really hurrying. From White Hand's demeanour it was apparent that the time for haste was already past.

Pearce said savagely: 'Now we know why Deakin slowed the train and set off that damned blasting charge – to distract our attention while Claremont dropped off the other side.'

'What worries me is the two things we don't know – *why* is White Hand here and how in the name of all that's holy did Deakin know he *would* be here?'

The Indians, guns lowered, now stood in a disconsolate group almost three hundred yards behind the train. Deakin, looking back, eased the throttle slightly.

'We've *got* to stop him.' The hysteria in Fairchild's voice was now unmistakable. 'We've got to, we've got to, we've got to! Look, we're hardly doing more than a walking pace. We can jump down, two on either side, out-flank him and —'

O'Brien said: 'And watch him wave goodbye as he opens the throttle wide?'

'You sure that's why he's going so slow?'

'What else?'

Claremont, his two riderless horses trailing, urged his horse up to the top of a narrow divide in a valley. Ahead of him, the rest of the troop of stampeding horses were now spread out, now gradually coming to a halt. Claremont reined in his horse at the top of the divide and looked into the middle distance. Less than three miles away, even through the still gently falling snow, the mouth of another valley could be seen branching off to the right. The telegraph poles issuing from the valley could be seen. It was the western exit of Breakheart Pass.

Claremont grimaced with pain and looked down at his bandaged left hand. Both it and a section of the rein it held were saturated with blood. He looked away and kicked his horse into motion.

The train was moving more quickly now, leaving the stationary Indians steadily further behind. White Hand, immobile and expressionless, watched the two scouts return from the pine wood. The leading scout said nothing, merely lifted his forearms, palms upwards. White Hand nodded and turned away. His men followed and they walked quickly, in double file, along the sleepers in the direction of the vanishing train.

Aboard the rear observation platform of the train Fairchild, O'Brien, Pearce and Henry looked acutely unhappy as they watched White Hand and his men becoming lost to sight round a bend in the track. Their unhappiness deepened further as they heard two pistol shots in rapid succession. Fairchild said, almost in despair: 'And what was that about?'

'Claremont, for a certainty.' Pearce spoke with conviction. 'Probably a signal to Deakin that he's driven White Hand's horses to hell and gone. Which means that White Hand's braves are going to have a long walk back to Fort Humboldt and by the time he gets there Deakin will be ready for him.'

'Sepp Calhoun will be there,' the Governor said hopefully.

'Calhoun has as much chance of coping with Deakin as my grandmother has,' Pearce said. 'Besides, he's usually half-drunk anyway.' His face tightened in a thin ugly line. 'What did I tell you? He's speeded up the train.'

No question, the train was accelerating. The four men looked at each other with even greater unease. O'Brien said: 'He's probably given up all hope of tricking us into jumping off.' He leaned out over the safety rail and looked ahead. There was a sharp crack and O'Brien jerked back into safety. He removed his hat with none too steady a hand and examined a jagged hole torn in the brim.

Pearce said drily: 'It would appear that he doesn't given up hope in other directions.'

Up front in the locomotive Deakin peered ahead

through the cab window. The snow had stopped now. The junction of the western exit of Breakheart Pass and the valley to his right – the agreed rendezvous with Claremont – was now less than two hundred yards away. Deakin said: 'Hold tight.' He closed the throttle and jammed on the brakes. The traction wheels locked to the accompaniment of the violent clanking of buffers crashing together. The four men on the rear platform regarded one another with a steadily increasing mixture of perplexity and apprehension. Deakin handed Banlon's gun to Marica, took the second tube of blasting powder from the tool-box.

The train ground to a standstill, Deakin said 'Now.' She stepped off the footplate and jumped, falling heavily, with an exclamation of pain, and rolling over several times. Deakin released the brake, put the lever in reverse and opened the throttle wide. Moments later he had joined Marica on the track-side.

It took the four men on the rear observation platform several minutes to realize that the train was moving backwards, not forwards. O'Brien, the first to recover, leaned out. His eyes widened as understanding came: Deakin, by the track-side, had his gun lined up on him: O'Brien had barely time to fling himself back even as the gun was fired.

'Jesus!' O'Brien used some choice language. 'They've jumped the train!'

'No one at the controls?' Fairchild was close to hysteria. 'For God's sake, jump off!'

O'Brien reached out a restraining hand. 'No!'

'God's sake, man, remember what happened to the troops in the runaways!'

'We need this train.' He pushed his way to the rear door of the leading coach. 'Drive a train, Nathan?'

Pearce shook his head.

'Me neither. I'll try.' He jerked a thumb forwards. 'Deakin.'

Pearce nodded and swung down from the platform. The train was already gathering speed and Pearce rolled over and over as he hit the track-side. But the steeply snow-covered slope of the embankment helped cushion his fall and he arrived at the bottom of the slope rather winded but unhurt. He rose at once to his feet and looked around.

The train, still accelerating, was already fifty yards away. Pearce glanced in the other direction where he could just see Deakin's head and shoulders; he was supporting a rather shaky Marica.

'This,' Deakin said, 'is just what I needed. Where are you hurt?'

'My ankle. And my wrist.'

'Can you stand?'

'I don't know. I don't think so.'

'Well, sit then.' He dumped her rather unceremoniously into a sitting position by the track-side. She favoured him with a very old-fashioned look, but Deakin's attention was already engaged elsewhere. Glancing back along the track, he could see that the train was already more than a quarter of a mile distant. What he could not see was O'Brien slithering down the cordwood in the tender and halting, his face an odd mixture of urgency and indecision as he found himself confronted with the baffling array of engine controls.

Deakin stooped and inserted the blasting-powder tube under a rail close to a sleeper. He tamped it all round with earth and stones, leaving only the fuse free.

Marica said in a noticeably cool tone: 'You're going to blow up the track?'

'That's the idea.'

'Not today, it's not.' Pearce advanced, Colt in hand. He glanced at Marica who was cradling her left wrist in her right hand. 'Maybe that'll teach you to jump off trains.' He closed on Deakin, ignoring Marica. 'Your gun. Under your coat. By the barrel, friend.'

Deakin reached under his coat. His gun came slowly into view.

Marica said: 'I've got a gun, too. Turn round, Marshal. Hands high.'

Pearce turned slowly, his eyes widening as he saw that Marica's right hand now cradled a revolver.

Deakin switched his grip on the barrel of his Colt. Pearce, who sensed what was coming, flung himself to one side, so that the blow lost some of its impact. But it was sufficient to make him stumble and fall, the gun coming free from his temporarily nerveless hand. He dived after it but Deakin was even quicker, jumping forward with his right foot swinging.

Marica winced in horror and revulsion at the sound of the heavy blow. She said in a whisper: 'You hit him when his back was turned, when his hands were up and then – and then –'

'And then I kicked him on the head. Next time you point a gun at a man like Pearce make sure the safety-catch is off.'

She stared at him, stared down at the gun in her hand, then shook her head slowly. After a moment she looked up.

'You might at least say thanks.'

'What? Oh, sure. Thanks.' He glanced down the track. The train, rapidly dwindling into the distance, was now going very quickly indeed and beginning to sway wildly. He switched his gaze. Claremont, two other horses held on loose reins, came cantering round the spur of a hill. At a gesture from Deakin he reined the horses in and held them where they were. Deakin dragged Pearce along the line, dropped him in unceremonious fashion, hurried back up the line, stooped, lit a fuse, picked up Marica and came quickly down the embankment. He helped her on to one of the spare horses, swung aboard the third himself and gestured that they should move away. After a short distance, as if by mutual consent, they stopped and looked back.

The explosion was curiously quiet. Rubble and dirt flew through the air. When those and the smoke settled, it could be seen that one sleeper was twisted and the left-hand line badly distorted.

Claremont said uncertainly: 'They can fix that, you know. They can unbolt the damaged section of the track, take it out and replace it with a section from behind the train.'

'I know. If I'd wrecked it permanently with a large charge, they'd have no option but to walk to the Fort.'

'Well?'

'That way they would arrive at the Fort alive, wouldn't they?'

Marica looked at him in horror.

'That means that we would all die.'

Marica's expression did not change.

'Don't you see?' Deakin's voice was gentle. 'I've no option.'

Marica shuddered and turned away. Deakin looked at her without expression, urged his horse into a canter. After a moment, the others followed.

TEN

O'Brien sagged against the side of the cab, mopping a sweat-stained brow in relief. The train was still reversing but, just as clearly, it was markedly slowing. O'Brien looked from the footplate towards the rear. White Hand and his men were now less than a quarter of a mile distant. For once, White Hand's iron impassivity had deserted him. His face reflected at first astonished disbelief, then gladness. He waved towards the train, beckoned to his men and broke into a run. Within two minutes the Paiutes were swarming aboard the stopped train while White Hand swung up on to the footplate to be greeted by O'Brien. Immediately, O'Brien opened the throttle and the train began to move forwards.

O'Brien said: 'And the horses were all gone?'

'All gone. And two of my men shot in the back. You have saved us a long walk, Major O'Brien. My friend, Marshal Pearce – I do not see him.'

'You will in a moment. He dropped off to attend to some urgent business.'

O'Brien peered ahead through the cab window where the western exit of Breakheart Pass could be seen coming up. Suddenly, to obtain a better view, he leaned out through the footplate entrance. Beyond question, there was a body lying on the track ahead: equally beyond question, the body was that of Pearce. O'Brien swore and jumped for the steam throttle and brake.

The train juddered to a halt. O'Brien and White Hand jumped down, ran forward, then stopped, grim-faced, at

the spectacle of the crumpled, bleeding and still very unconscious Pearce. As one, both men lifted their eyes and
looked about thirty yards ahead. Above a hole blown in
the rail-bed, a sleeper was twisted and a rail badly
buckled.

White Hand said softly: 'Deakin will die for this.'

O'Brien looked at him for a long moment, then said
sombrely: 'Not if he sees you first, White Hand.'

'White Hand fears no man.'

'Then you'd better learn to fear this one. He is a
United States Federal agent. In your own language, he
has the cunning of a serpent and the luck of the devil.
Marshal Pearce can count himself lucky that Deakin did
not choose to kill him. Come, let us repair this track.'

Under O'Brien's direction it took the Paiutes all of
twenty minutes to effect the repair. They worked in two
gangs – one removing the damaged section of the track,
another freeing a sound section to the rear of the train.
The damaged section was thrown down the embankment
while the undamaged section was brought forward from
the rear and fitted in its place. Bedding down the sleepers
and aligning the track was no job for unskilled amateurs
but eventually O'Brien was satisfied that, jerry-built
though the improvisation was, it might just bear the
weight of the train. During the operation a groaning
Pearce, his back propped against the cow-catcher, slowly
regained consciousness, supported by a solicitous Henry
who constantly dabbed a cheek and temple already badly
cut and spectacularly bruised.

'We go now,' O'Brien said. The Paiutes, Pearce and
Henry went back into the main body of the train while
White Hand rejoined O'Brien in the cab. O'Brien released the brake and opened the throttle very gently
indeed, at the same time peering out gingerly over the

side. As the locomotive wheels reached the new section of the track the line dipped slightly but not dangerously. When the last of the coaches had passed over the damaged area O'Brien returned to the controls and opened the throttles wide.

Deakin, Claremont and Marica had stopped, all three still on horseback. Deakin was swiftly rebandaging Claremont's gory hand.

Claremont said urgently : 'Minutes count, man ! We're losing time.'

'We'll lose you if we don't stop this bleeding.' He glanced at Marica, who with set face and lips compressed against the pain, held her left wrist tightly in her right hand. 'How's it going?'

'I'll be all right.'

Deakin looked at her briefly, without expression, then resumed the rebandaging. They had scarcely moved on when he looked at her again. She was slumped in the saddle, her head bowed. He said : 'Is your wrist that bad?'

'It's my ankle. I can't put my foot in the stirrup.' Deakin moved round to the other side of her horse. Her left leg was dangling clear of the stirrup. He looked away, turned around and glanced upward over his right shoulder. The snow was gone and the clouds drifting away to leave the washed-out blue of the sky; the sun was appearing over the shoulder of a mountain. Again, he looked at Marica : with ankle and wrist out of commission she was now scarcely able to maintain her seat in the saddle. He pulled in close to her horse, lifted her across to his own, took the reins of the now riderless horse in his free hand and urged both animals into a rapid canter. Claremont, who looked in no better case han Marica, followed close behind. They were now paralleling the line of the railway track. The ground here was flat and relatively free from snow and they made comparatively good time.

Sepp Calhoun was in his usual place, the Commandant's chair, with his feet in their usual position, the Commandant's table, pursuing his usual custom which was drinking the Commandant's whisky and smoking one of his cheroots. The only other occupant of the room was Colonel Fairchild, who sat on a straight deal chair and had his wrists bound behind him. The door opened and a scruffy and very swarthy white man entered.

Calhoun said genially: 'All right, Carmody?'

'Fixed. The telegraphists are locked up with the rest. Benson is at the gate. Harris is fixing some grub.'

'Fine. Just time for a snack before our friends arrive. Less than an hour, I should say.' He grinned mockingly at Fairchild. 'The battle of Breakheart Pass belongs to history now, Colonel.' He smiled even more broadly. 'I guess "massacre" is the word I'm looking for.'

In the supply wagon a still badly battered but much recovered Pearce was busy handing out repeaters and ammunition to the Paiutes who crowded round him. There was no sign of the traditional Indian reserve. They chattered and smiled and their eyes shone, children transported by their new toys. Pearce made his way forward and clambered into the tender, three Winchester repeaters under his arm. He passed into the cab and handed one to White Hand.

'A present for you, White Hand.'

The Indian smiled. 'You are a man of your word, Marshal Pearce.'

Pearce made to smile but his face at once felt so painful that he rapidly thought better of it. Instead he said: 'Twenty minutes. Not more than twenty minutes.'

Deakin had fifteen minutes on them. Momentarily he halted the horses and gazed ahead. The bridge over the ravine was no more than half a mile away; immediately beyond that lay the Fort Humboldt compound. He helped Marica on to her own horse and motioned for both her and Claremont to precede him. He drew his pistol and held it in his hand. In now brilliant sunshine the three horses picked their delicate way across the trestle bridge that spanned the ravine and cantered up to the compound gate. Benson, the guard, a man with a dull, stupid, brutalized face, moved out to intercept them, cocked rifle ready in his hands.

'Who are you?' His voice was slurred with a mixture of truculence and alcohol. 'What's your business at Fort Humboldt?'

'Not with you.' Deakin's voice was bleak, authoritative. 'Sepp Calhoun. Quickly!'

'Who you got there?'

'Are you blind? Prisoners. From the train.'

'From the train?' Benson nodded uncertainly, whatever mental processes he had clearly in temporary abeyance. 'You'd better come.'

Benson led them across the compound. As they approached the Commandant's office the door opened and Calhoun appeared, a gun in either hand. He said savagely: 'Who the hell you got there, Benson?'

'Says they're from the train, boss.'

Deakin ignored both Calhoun and Benson and moved his pistol in the direction of Claremont and Marica. 'Get down, you two.' He turned to Calhoun. 'You Calhoun?

Let's talk inside.'

Calhoun levelled both pistols at Deakin. 'Uh-uh. Too fast, mister. Who are you?'

Deakin said in weary exasperation. 'John Deakin. Nathan Pearce sent me.'

'So you say.'

'So *they* say.' He nodded to the now dismounted and clearly sick Claremont and Marica. 'My passport. Hostages. Safe-conduct. Call them what you like. Nathan said I was to take them for proof.'

A shade less aggressively Calhoun said : 'I've seen passports in better shape.'

'They tried to be clever. Meet Colonel Claremont, the relief Commandant. And Miss Marica Fairchild – the present Commandant's daughter.'

Calhoun's eyes widened, his mouth opened perceptibly and his guns momentarily wavered, but his recovery was almost immediate. 'We'll soon see about that. Inside.' He and Benson ushered the other three, at gun-point, into the Commandant's office.

Colonel Fairchild stared as the door opened. Despite the bound hands, he stumbled shakily to his feet.

'Marica! Marica! And Colonel Claremont.' Marica hobbled across the room and threw her arms around him. 'My dear, my dear. What have they done to you? And what – what in God's name – why are you here?'

Deakin said to Calhoun : 'Satisfied?'

'Well, I guess – but I never heard of no John Deakin.'

Deakin thrust his gun inside his coat, a pacific gesture which helped further reassure the wavering Calhoun.

'Who do you think took those four hundred rifles from the Winchester armoury?' He had the ascendancy now and used it with savage authority. 'God's sake, man, stop wasting time. Things are bad, terribly bad. Your precious

White Hand botched the job. He's dead. So's O'Brien. Pearce is hurt, badly. The soldiers have the train and when they get it going again – '

'White Hand, O'Brien, Pearce – '

Deakin nodded curtly to Benson. 'Tell him to wait outside.'

'Outside?' Calhoun seemed dazed.

'Out. There's worse to come – but for your ears only.'

Calhoun nodded mechanically at a bewildered Benson, who left, closing the door behind him.

Calhoun said despairingly: 'There couldn't *be* anything worse – '

'Yes, there is. This.' The pistol was back in Deakin's hand, the muzzle pressing with brutal force against Calhoun's teeth. Deakin swiftly relieved the stupefied Calhoun of both guns and handed one to Claremont, who lined it up on Calhoun. Deakin produced a knife and sliced the bonds of Colonel Fairchild, who was no less flabbergasted than Calhoun, and laid Calhoun's other gun on the table beside him. 'Yours. When you're fit to use it. How many other men does Calhoun have? Apart from Benson?'

'Who in God's name are you? How – '

Deakin grabbed Fairchild's lapels. 'How – many – men?'

'Two. Carmody and Harris, they're called.'

Deakin wheeled round and dug the muzzle of his Colt violently into Calhoun's kidneys. Calhoun gasped with pain. Deakin repeated the process. He said, smiling: 'You have the blood of scores of men on your hands, Calhoun. Please, please believe me that I'm just begging for the excuse to kill you.' From the expression on Calhoun's face it was apparent that he believed him totally.

'Tell Benson that you want him, Carmody and Harris here at once.'

Deakin opened the door slightly and prodded Calhoun towards the opening. Benson was pacing up and down only a few feet away.

Calhoun said hoarsely: 'Get Carmody and Harris here. And yourself. Now!'

'What's up, boss? You look – you look like death.'

'God's sake, man, hurry!'

Benson hesitated, then ran across the compound. Deakin closed the door and said to Calhoun: 'Turn round.'

Calhoun obeyed. Deakin's reversed gun swung and he caught Calhoun before he toppled to the ground. Marica stared at him in horror.

'Spare me your goddamned lectures.' Deakin's tone was coldly conversational. 'A minute from now and he would have been as desperate as a cornered rat.' He turned to Fairchild. 'How many survivors?'

'We lost only ten men – and they gave a good account of themselves.' Fairchild was still trying to massage life back into his hands. 'The rest were caught in their bunks. Calhoun and his friends – we'd given the damned renegades lodging for the night – overpowered my night guards and let the Indians in. But they're two miles from here, in an abandoned mine, with Indian guards.'

'No matter. I don't need them. I don't want them. Last thing I want is a pitched battle. How you feeling now?'

'A great deal better, Mr Deakin. What do you want me to do?'

'When I give the word, go to the armoury and get me a sackful of blasting powder and fuses. Please be very quick then. Where are your cells?'

Fairchild pointed. 'The corner of the compound there.'

'The key?'

Fairchild took a key from the board behind his desk and handed it to Deakin, who nodded his thanks, pocketed it and took up a watching post by the window.

He had to watch only for seconds. Benson, Carmody and Harris were crossing the compound at a dead run. At a nod from Deakin, Claremont helped him to drag the prostrate Calhoun into a more or less standing position. As the three running men approached the Commandant's office the door opened wide and the unconscious form of Calhoun was pushed violently down the steps. The confusion was immediate and complete and the tangled heap of Benson, Carmody and Harris had nothing to offer in the way of resistance when Deakin, gun in hand, appeared in the doorway. Fairchild appeared immediately behind him and ran across to the opposite side of the compound. Deakin followed, leading his horse by one hand while with the other, Colt in hand, he shepherded the other three, now bearing the inert Calhoun, towards the cells. As he turned the key on them, Fairchild appeared from a nearby doorway, carrying what appeared to be a fairly heavy sack. Deakin, on horseback now, snatched up the sack, slung it across the pommel of his saddle and, urging his horse to a gallop, swung left through the main gateway of the compound. Marića, supported by a still shaky Claremont, the blind leading the blind, appeared from the Commandant's office. Together with Fairchild, they made their best speed towards the gateway.

Deakin pulled up his horse in the concealment of an outcrop of rock that had been blasted to make the approach to the trellis bridge, dismounted, flung the bag over his shoulder and headed for the bridge.

Pearce swung out from the left-hand cab window of the locomotive cab and looked ahead. A wide smile crossed his sadly battered face.

'We're there!' Exultation in his voice. 'We're almost there!'

White Hand joined him by the window. The trellis bridge was less than a mile ahead. White Hand smiled and lovingly rubbed the stock of his Winchester repeater.

Deakin, meantime, had just finished wedging two large charges of blasting powder between the wooden piers and buttresses of the trellis bridge, one on either side. He had used scarcely half of the powder Fairchild had given him, but estimated the quantity to be sufficient. He shinned up a wooden buttress, threw the half-empty sack on to the track, then cautiously raised his head; the train was now no more than a quarter of a mile distant. He descended swiftly, ignited the fuses of both charges, then climbed as swiftly back on to the bridge. The train was no more than two hundred yards distant. Deakin shouldered his bag and ran back to the western exit of the bridge.

Pearce and White Hand, leaning out from opposite sides of the footplate, saw the fleeing figure of Deakin just clearing the bridge. Momentarily, the two men in the cab stared at each other, then simultaneously raised their Winchesters. Bullets struck the ground and ricocheted off the rocks near the flying figure of Deakin, but because of the latter's dodging, twisting run and the most unstable firing platform provided by the swaying locomotive, none came too close. Within seconds Deakin had thrown himself behind the shelter of the outcrop of rock.

'The bridge!' Pearce's voice was almost a scream. 'The devil's mined the bridge!' O'Brien, his face masked in rage and fear, slammed shut the throttle and jammed on the brakes. But the train, though abruptly slowing, was already on the bridge.

Fairchild, Claremont and Marica, now no more than two hundred yards distant, stopped and stared. The train appeared to be almost across the bridge; the locomotive and tender were, in fact, already across the bridge and on solid rock. O'Brien, at the controls, mouthing incomprehensible words, realized that he had made a mistake, possibly even a fatal one, released the brake and opened the throttle to its widest extent. But O'Brien was too late. There came two almost simultaneous white flashes, a double roar that combined into one and the bridge disintegrated and collapsed into the ravine. The three coaches disappeared at once into the depths of the gorge, dragging the still coupled tender and locomotive after them. The tender had already disappeared and the locomotive was fast following them when three figures, all bearing Winchesters, jumped clear from the cab and landed heavily on the solid rock. The locomotive was dragged inexorably over the edge and amid the rending screech of tearing metal and the splintering of heavy baulks of timber, the entire train dropped into the depths.

Shaken, but still going concerns, Pearce, O'Brien and White Hand scrambled to their feet. With the three men lining their guns on him Deakin seemed momentarily paralysed, then dived for safety without a shot being fired. Shock had slowed the reactions of the men with the Winchesters.

Fairchild, Claremont and Marica flung themselves flat as the three men advanced, their Winchesters cocked. Deakin thrust his hand under his coat. It came out slowly, empty. His gun was in the Commandant's room. The three men were now less than fifteen yards distant from him, rounding the outcrop: it was obvious that Deakin had no gun. But in his right hand he held an already ignited tube of blasting powder. He waited for what seemed a dangerously long period, then threw it over the outcrop.

The charge exploded over the three men, momentarily blinding them and throwing them off balance. Deakin ran round the corner of the outcrop. There was much smoke and dust but he could see that White Hand, his hands clutched to his streaming eyes, had lost his rifle. Two seconds later it was in Deakin's hands, lined up on the still slightly dazed Pearce and O'Brien.

Deakin said: '*Don't* do it. *Don't* make me make history. *Don't* make me the first man in history to kill another with a Winchester repeater.'

Pearce, who had recovered the most quickly of the three, hurled himself to one side, bringing up his repeater. Deakin's gun boomed.

Deakin said: 'I think that's enough history for one day.'

O'Brien nodded and threw down his gun. His tear-filled eyes could barely see.

The three of them were joined by Fairchild, Marica and Claremont, the last with a very steady gun in his wounded hand. Deakin, Fairchild and Marica stood a little apart close to the edge of the shattered bridge, gazing downwards. Far below in the depths of the ravine lay the crumpled, broken remains of the train with the locomotive lying on top of the crushed coaches. There was no movement to be seen, no sign of life.

Deakin said heavily: 'An eye for an eye. Well, I suppose we have the ones who matter – O'Brien, Calhoun and White Hand.'

Fairchild was sombre. 'All except one.'

Deakin looked at him. 'You – you know about your brother?'

'I always suspected. I never knew. He – he was the ringleader?'

'O'Brien was. O'Brien used him, used his greed and his weakness.'

'And all his ambition, all his greed, ends in the bottom of a ravine.'

'For him, for you, for your daughter – the best way.'

'And now?'

'One detachment of your men to bring back the horses I abandoned down the line. Another to repair the telegraph line. Then we call up a train-load of army and civil engineers to rebuild this bridge.'

Marica said: 'And you'll be returning to Reese City now?'

'I'll be going back to Reese City when that bridge is repaired and a train has crossed it to load all the bullion in Fort Humboldt. I'll let that gold and silver out of my sight when it's reached Washington. But not before.'

Fairchild said: 'But it'll take weeks to repair that bridge.'

'Like enough.'

Marica smiled. 'It looks like being a long hard winter.'

Deakin smiled in return. 'Oh, I don't know. I dare say we'll find something to talk about.'